PRAXIS

by Robert B. Midgett

Same Old Story Publishing

VICTOR FERUS, PRESIDENT and CEO

SAME OLD STORY PRODUCTIONS

Mount Juliet, Tennessee

Halfway, Oregon

PRAXIS

"To my friend Santiago Cirillo, my former English teacher and present friend, Josh Mauthe . . .

"And finally to my dearest M. Davies, who has been through it all."

This is the second novel in the Vagabonds Universe.

*Special thanks to Mom, Dad, Aunt Jeanna,
Mira and Sherryl!*

ACT ONE

1

Allun

The name Vortigan is not a fucking joke.

The name Vortigan means the fucking world to entire cities of people. The name Vortigan is a determining factor of who lives and who dies, in many places. When you hear the name Vortigan and you do not tremble, you're either a Vortigan yourself, a soldier or servant of the Vortigans, or you're a dead man. The Vortigan family has been around for a long, long time--it ain't gonna die out anytime soon. Despite our old Justicar dying--rest my little boy's soul--we do have a new one. She's goddamn efficient, too.

Regardless of the fact that the Vortigan name is not something to fuck with, many people attempt it. These attempts are all in vain.

I rush quickly down the street, a holdout blaster-rifle stuffed under my coat. My hair flows behind me. My overcoat flaps in the wind. The rain falls down and makes the whole sidewalk wet. I make my best effort not to slip as I run, hearing the sirens blare around me. Several Sar Vort hospital trucks go zipping past me. I can see the reflection of my bright glowing eyes in the rainwater that paves my path. My curly black hair is flattening as it gets damper. I still can't believe someone had the balls to do it. On a Tartuan midnight, when all were asleep, a bomb was planted at a Vortigan compound. A truck blew. A fire burned away the lives of several Vortigan family and friends.

I just got the news and I will use this news to my advantage. The ones who did it will pay very dearly. I turn down the winding road up to the compound, sliding out my blaster-rifle. A Delkyrian blade is strapped to my leg. If I can get any of the poor, dumb bastards alive, they're sure as hell not going to be a problem for us further. I can only think back to what my mom said before I rushed out: "make them beg." *I will, Ma.* I consider our enemies, the Dreadwals. the Tennus family. I always fucking hated both of them, but hatred ain't good for survival when the ones you hate are as big as you.

I see the fire, burning brighter than the eyes in my skull. Ambulances, firemen, Vortigan police--everyone surrounds the main house. I rush forward, toward several police officers in a cluster around a man. At first, I suspect it may be a Vortigan soldier or associate that was wounded, but I find the reality to be worse than that, a living assailant. I clear out the police and smack the man across the face with the butt of my rifle. "Where the fuck did you come from?"

"I... I can't..."

"Where are the others?" I put my boot to his face roughly, forcing him to turn completely over. He lies flat on his back, whimpering as I move my foot to his throat. He screams for help, but no one comes for him. I'm the highest authority in Sar Vort, right under Ma, so he's not getting shit. I press down a little harder. "Where are the others?" I ask again.

"O... Over-"

He hesitates. I swipe my foot across his face again. His nose is bubbling blood as he tries to breathe. I put my foot back on his throat and he tenses up. I stare directly into his pathetic, fading eyes. He clenches them shut and lets out a yelp. "Over the back fence!" He screams out in submission.

"You sure?" I ask him, pushing a bit harder.

"I'm sure!" He yells, scared shitless.

I press down with my boot until I hear a crack. He begins flailing, tugging at his throat, hoping for some form of help. He's not getting any.

As he suffocates behind me, I rush for the fence. The police surround him again, chattering as they see me make my sprint. I begin climbing the fence as nimbly as I can. Despite that I'm not the man I once was. Behind the compound is a planted forest, just for the soldier-boys to enjoy. I'd have taken the gate, but it's a whole process just to get through. I fire a shot into the tall, dark woods.

The shine of the blast reveals beautiful pink leaves, which once flourished on Tartarus. All animals are domestic now, as all trees are planted. I like it just fine, though. We've got our nature under control. More than can be said for other worlds.

I begin letting out a whistle, trying to get an indication of where the bomber might be. Whistling will play with his head. Calling out, firing shots. Making him think that I know where the hell he is. Maybe he'll come out flailing, but I ain't leaving this forest until one of us is dead.

I let off a shot again. "Come on, shithead!" I let one off into the air and it fizzles away as it reaches the distance.

"I ain't gonna bite!" I say humorously, but I don't laugh. Laughing ain't something a lot of people can make me do, including myself. Only man ever to make me laugh was my brother Alex. Man, he's gonna shit a brick when he hears about this. I fire again and again, in separate directions. "I know where you are! No sense in hiding!" I hear a scamper in the back of the woods. Bet he didn't anticipate the back wall being too high to climb. Lucky for me, the trees are too flimsy to climb. I bet he's going to try, though. Poor, poor sack of shit.

"Come out right now--maybe I won't kill you!" I walk through the grassy flatland quietly, like a hunter. I don't know how I haven't seen this bastard's eyes yet. A Tartuan's eyes stick out so blatantly it's almost sad. We don't make for the stealthiest of people. I consider, then, that his assistant isn't a Tartuan. Perhaps an Astarian slave, I think, but that's likely incorrect. An Astarian couldn't jump that fence. Hell, an Alkin probably would've been caught by now due to the fact that any Alkin in this city that ain't a Vortigan isn't coming onto the Vortigan compound. I wonder what that bastard told them to let him on.

I let off a shot when I hear another ruffle of leaves. I can see the vague shape of his leg. He's trying to climb the tree. I fire a little bit left, hoping to blow the bastard to hell.

It nearly hits. Another shot. I hear a scream and a crash, followed by the cracking of twigs. Further yells. Sobbing.

I finally see the well-hidden glow in his eyes. I lean over him when I get near, smiling as he claws away the ground, trying to pull himself as far from me as he can get. I pop a shot into his other leg. He yelps again.

"Who the fuck do you think you are?"

"Please, please, no!" He screeches, trying fruitlessly to pull himself onward with just his hands.

I shake my head and blew a hole in his right hand. Through the crying and flailing, I do manage to get him to turn over. He stares at me just as pathetically as the last guy.

"Who the hell hired you, eh?" I begin to pull my Delkyrian blade from my leg. He shakes his head and cries out. "I'll cut the information out of you."

"No! No!"

He doesn't budge, it seems. Well, he may be a piece of shit, but I admire his will. I bury the blade into his gut, twisting it.

"Fuck! No! No!" He screams even louder than he was prior to the stabbing.

I sigh and, out of a sick sense of pity that disgusts even myself, I slice his throat. Too good for the bastard. He bleeds out faster than I wanted him to, but I suppose that's what you call making the right choice.

I shake my head and turn back to see several police officers rushing into the forest. I shake my head as I walk on, my blade back in its sheathe and my hands tucked away in my pockets.

"You ain't making any arrests tonight, boys."

* * * *

"They're dead, Ma." I say as I light up a smoke, imported from Earth.

My mother's voice erupts from the comm system in my car, fuzzy and almost unrecognizable.

"I stomped the first fucker's throat. Cut the other one's."

"Did you find out who planted the bomb, Allun?" Ma asks me as I pull down the road for the Vortigan mansion. The guards at the gate give me a nod and one flips a switch, sliding the gate door open. "Allun?"

"No, Ma, sorry. We might need some aid on this." I groan and reach over to the fifth of whiskey at my side. I take a large gulp and pull in, parking my car in the garage, just beside Ma's. Just beyond Ma's big, black, weaponized rover of a truck is my sister Orvia's far smaller blue speed-demon of a two-seater.

I step out of my car and walk in through the door from the garage into the mansion living area. A bull rakia's head is mounted just above Ma's armchair. It has a snarling expression and an air of menace to it, as well as a large, scaly snout and thin, narrow eyes. This particular bull rakia was killed by Ma herself on a hunting trip.

"Allun!" I hear a pleasant voice call out and light, fast footsteps, followed by the creaking of the floor under heavier, slower footsteps. Orvia emerges from the doorway, running to me and grinning. I embrace her warmly, which is more than I can say for how I handle most people. She squeezes me tight, kissing me on the cheek and eventually letting me go again. I smile--again, more than I can say for how I handle most people--and give her a kiss on the cheek back.

"Orvia!" I say excitedly. "How's my favorite baby sister?"

"Your favorite? What about Iria?" She asks. I laugh.

"She's my *other* favorite baby sister."

I didn't anticipate a visit from Orvia, so I imagine she just arrived. Ma enters the room with a weary smile. She's much heavier, in contrast to Orvia. Ma is built like a wall, while Orvia is more like a twig. They both have the same rounded face, though; it may compliment Orvia more, however. It's worse when my aunts visit. The house is filled to the brim with curly-haired, round-faced tough old women.

"So what brings you back home, sis?" I ask her as I head over to the couch, taking a seat and looking into the mesmerizing fireplace.

Ma takes a seat at her armchair and has Orvia take a seat in the chair beside her own. "Last I checked, you ain't handling business."

"Last I checked, neither were you." Orvia snaps, offended by my statement. She gets over it quickly, though, giving me another bright smile. "Ma invited me back a few weeks ago. Just got around to coming here."

"And you didn't tell me, Ma?" I say, genuinely upset.

She just shakes her head and gives me a knowing smile. It's a look I've come to know well. A look that says, 'We'll talk later.' Ma's been giving me that look a lot lately. "Well, Orvia, it's nice to have you back home for a little while."

* * * *

"It's dangerous out there for such a mouse of a girl."

Ma puffs on her cigar and flips through a big book on the desk in her study. I close the door behind us so Orvia doesn't hear. The room is dim, the only light on is coming from over Ma's desk. She doesn't like to have too many lights on. The study is a wide room, with bookshelves lining each wall. Ma collects books from all kinds of worlds. Earth, Tartarus, Suregua, Astar--back before Astar was turned into a big workhouse--Alkineth, even some of the Outer-Worlds.

"If she were like me, or any of your aunts, we wouldn't need to call her back every time there was trouble."

"You knew there would be trouble that far back?" I ask, shocked that Ma wouldn't have said something sooner to hopefully prevent this whole, horrible ordeal.

Ma shakes her head as she reaches behind her desk, pulls a bottle and pours herself a glass of Old Tartarus Liquor.

"I didn't know there would be a bombing. I figured someone would end up trying to kidnap her, ransom her off, rape her... There are a lot of bad people out there, Allun." Ma pours me a glass as well, sliding it to the end of the desk.

I pick it up slowly, staring into her big, bright white eyes. "*We're* some of those bad people, Ma." I add as I down the shot, putting my glass back down on the desk as she pours me another one.

"Don't think I don't know it." Ma slides open her drawer, pulling a small revolver from Earth. She places it down gently and carefully on the end of the desk, beckoning me toward it.

I pick it up, inspecting it. Snub-nose .38.

Ma wants me to send a message. "We've gotta be bad people to keep our position, Allun. Now I want you to find the limp-dicked little prick that arranged that bombing and put a bullet in his head. I want you to send a message."

"Gonna need some help, ain't we, Ma? Typically, family shouldn't handle justicar business on their own. If we do, what's the point in having one?" I tuck the gun away in the back of my pants, hidden under my thick, still damp coat.

"Call for her, then, if you can get over what happened." Mom states, turning my mind to tears and anger.

I clench my fists and remove my coat slowly, placing it down on the chair across from her. I turn away, staring into the mirror on the wall beside the door. I begin rolling up the sleeves of my black button-down and straightening my suspenders, doing anything and everything to keep my mind off of the sheer anger that overcomes me every time she mentions the incident. My poor, poor boy; killed under order of my own big brother. "Ma..." I start to say, but I know she'll protest. "I ain't calling Taius."

"You've gotta get in touch with him if you want anything to get done, Allun. What happened to Walder was a necessary action on his part. We both know it."

Ma breaks my heart every time she talks about it. She's so cold and unfeeling when it comes to my boy. My youngest boy. My last would-be-living boy. "He was my grandson. It pains me to say it, but he was awful. He wasn't fit for his job or even... Well, for the family."

"You shut the fuck up." I say quietly, my heart thumping. I turn to face her, tears starting to pour down my face. "You shut the fuck up about my son."

"I understand your feelings." Ma stands from her desk, moving around it and coming toward me. She paces slowly, refined. She reaches me and stares into my eyes, placing her hand over my mouth and silencing me. "But you will not do this. You will not disgrace our family by talking down to its matriarch. You will call Taius and you will tell him that we need his Justicar."

His Justicar. I don't like that. She removes her hand from my mouth.

"Yes, Ma."

"Good."

2

Praxis

Blue. The color blue drips from the walls, the ceiling, floods all around the floor. A room of Alkin--all young, stupid, innocent--are drowning in it. I am just one among the crowd, just one body among many.

If I die, perhaps I'll be missed. Or perhaps not. It honestly doesn't matter at this point. All I'm worried about is my own survival. I float to the top of the rising blue, while people below clamber and grab at one another, all trying to swim, all unable to. I gasp and try to breathe. The blue tastes coppery and acidic, thickening as it rises. I scream as a hand grabs my ankle. I kick at the face of the Alkin it's attached to.

I continue to swim until I'm near the top. The room will close off. There's no escape from it, either. We'll all drown in the pool of blue. The bodies already begin floating.

I start pushing them together and try to make something to steady myself. I clumsily hoist myself over the corpses. I worry that they're going to sink, but they don't seem to. I lie atop them, safe for only a moment.

The blue continues to rise until I'm pressed against the ceiling. It stops in what seems to be a miracle. I make a push at the ceiling and begin to see cracking. Pushing and pushing, I begin to make a dent in the top of the room.

I break through it in a display of strength. I climb over and stare down. I am the only one in the room to survive. Dead Alkin float around in the room beneath me. I stand in a void now, staring at a floor that seems to span on much farther than the room.

I walk and walk, not knowing where to go. The floor is unmarked and gray, a cold and metallic looking platform. I can hear how hollow it is under certain areas though, giving me the sense that perhaps there are other rooms. I stare ahead of me and see something, a large figure, muscular, unnatural. A silhouette.

It stomps toward me, its arms outstretched. I move away from it, fearfully. I don't know my reasoning, but the being seems bad.

I gasp as I wake. I'm cold, having thrown my blankets off of the side of my bed, covered in sweat and feeling a sense of impending doom.

I stare at the closet, knowing that nothing is there. Still, it always helps to check. I reach over the side of my mattress and unzip a hidden compartment, sliding out a tiny wooden drawer. I grab a blaster-pistol from the inside and hold it for my own sense of security. I take a deep breath and let out an exhausted sigh.

A pretty young slave lies down beside me, his naked body as cold as mine. He seems to be asleep still. I give him a kiss on the forehead and put the blanket over him, tossing on some sleepwear and stepping out.

Sometimes I think I'm still on Alkineth when I awake. Sometimes I wish I was a young girl again, that I was still on my home-world and that everyone was alright. That all of this has been a prolonged, fucked up dream.

But I know better than that. Sometimes I question Proscriptus. I question whether or not I was meant to come here. I wish I could change the past, but I'm no more capable of that than anyone else. I've considered leaving before, but the thought always passes. What else is for me out there?

I've taken to having slaves keep me company. Only the ones that don't seem to mind it, though. The last thing I want to do is make slaves *feel* like slaves.

I step outside and yawn, stretching and popping my neck. I see, outside of my bed chamber, two Delkyrian guards with swords at their hips. They wear well-crafted armor from their respective clans and looks of determination on their faces. I consider the possibility of convincing one of *them* to keep me company. I'm certainly not opposed to taking on other races occasionally.

"You boys alright?" I ask casually, glancing between the pair.

They don't smile or frown, but keep their determined looks. They nod, avoiding eye-contact with me. "Just because I'm a Vortigan Justicar doesn't mean you have to be so formal."

"Delkyrians, right?" I hear Alex's voice break through the room.

I glance back to see him standing in the kitchen, pouring himself a drink from my cabinet. He's far too comfortable in my house. The grizzled old man's been growing out his beard in a specific spot, giving him a thick white goatee. The years haven't been kind to his appearance. He smirks, gazing at the two young Delkyrian men in front of my door. "They'll do whatever you tell 'em, except 'act casual.'"

"Alex!" I gasp, both at the racism of that remark and the fact that he entered my house without permission. His old gray eyes still have a glimmer of youth, but his motions are forced. He's obviously not the man of action he once was. "What the hell are you doing in my house?" He sips from one of my wine glasses that he's helped himself to and makes his way around the counter, taking a seat on my couch. I can almost hear his bones pop as he leans forward to sit the glass down.

"We've got some trouble." He says vaguely, urging me to take a seat beside him. He stares at the TV that I appear to have left running in the night.

We both stare at the large flat screen once I take a seat beside him, watching the muted images of corpses on the Tartuan news. A row of corpses, all burned to different degrees; some beyond recognition, some only partially. They're all dead, though. Every corpse I've seen on TV lately has been real. "Sar Vort--you know about Sar Vort, right?"

"What do you mean by that?" I ask him, seeing the name of another Tartuan city appear on the TV. "I know a little about it. I know the Vortigans are the head family in charge of it. I know that it's got one of the highest organized crime rates on Tartarus."

"That about covers it." He tells me, sipping from his wine glass. No, *my* wine glass. The bastard didn't even think to offer me one of my own damned drinks. "Well, we have some trouble on Sar Vort."

"Get your thumb out of your ass and tell me what the trouble is." I bark, getting irritable. "You're walking me in circles here."

He frowns and gives me a look of displeasure, noticing that I've taken to snapping at him more as my age has progressed. I haven't meant to, and I've tried to change it, but the fact of the matter is that he's only gotten weaker and repetitive and I've only gotten a need for business. If the old bastard wants to waste time, he should waste his own.

"A Vortigan compound on Sar Vort was bombed." He takes a gulp from the glass and leans back, relaxing himself despite the worried look in his eyes. "We don't know who did it. We don't even know the motive. The only two people we could have questioned were killed by Allun when he caught them."

"Crucified Christ." I shake my head in disapproval.

Allun Vortigan is a name I can't match to a face. Despite having never met him, I hear a world of conversations about him. From the sound of it, he's a nihilist. He appears to be destructive and dangerous, a constant threat to himself and to those around him. "So, what, you want me to leave Proscriptus and go to Sar Vort?"

He shrugs lightly, not making a big motion for it. He hasn't made big motions with his arms since he was shot on our first day in Proscriptus. God, was that a life-changing day...

"I mean..." He hesitates, as if what he plans on saying next will offend me. "We haven't decided on it yet. I still need to talk to Taius, but you will more than likely be going."

He expects me to lash out, which I almost do, but I catch myself beforehand. I'm not going to keep barking at Alex. He's the man who raised me and I won't allow myself to disrespect him too much.

"I needed an excuse but I... I mostly wanted to see how you've been holding up."

"I'm fine." I lie, reaching into the cigar box on my table. I pull one out and light it up with a shiny silver lighter I left right next to it. I puff and inhale, leaning back into a recumbent state, much like his.

He points over to a pile of bottles in the corner I forgot to throw away and shakes his head, giving a bit of a sleepier smile than is typical of him.

"People who are fine typically don't drink alone." He says dismally, knowing the feeling just as well as I do.

He gulps down the last bit of wine, as if he's telling me his own feelings much more subtly. I run my eyes over the guards, mentally undressing them, entertaining myself while I think about what I could say in retort to Alex so that there isn't any awkward silence between us.

I glance back at the TV screen. Two young Tartuan men hold guns at each others heads. It's a drama, one of those low-budget crime shows that are all so common on late night TV. A young, handsome man and an older, balding, but still just as handsome man, shoot at each other. A cutaway to a woman screaming, wounded. A blaster-mark is made on her, but not a realistic one.

"Who says I've been drinking alone?" I ask with a sly smirk, glancing over at the bedrooms past the imaginary nudity of my guards. Beyond that door, a slave lies sleeping--quite peacefully.

I wish I could have his peace of mind in sleep. Somehow a slave is happier than I am. It saddens me to think about, but I can't really do anything. Therapists typically aren't common on Proscriptus, despite the apparent need for them. Most people don't want to meet with the messed up killers of this station.

"Your eyes say it." He gazes into them, but I can't look back at him without avoiding eye contact.

I ash my cigar and shake my head, continuing to examine the TV screen. A young police woman--showing far too much cleavage for a cop--fires a blaster-pistol at a criminal. He goes down quickly, but he doesn't appear to be dead. Quickly, more supposed criminals rush out of the building behind him. The police woman hides behind her car, calling in for more backup.

My attention turns back to Alex when his voice breaks the silence again. "I'm fine." I repeat myself, now undressing the characters on TV with my eyes. I picture the older man to be muscular, despite being at an age when people tend to let themselves go. The older man shot the younger man, leaving him dead on the ground. The older man is supposed to be a cop. If he were a good one, he wouldn't abandon a scene like that so quickly. Media depicts sentient life as something to be tossed away. I honestly can't tell if that's a heartless exception or the heartless truth.

"You know, saving you was probably the best choice I ever made." Alex gets even more emotional, smiling. He slides his hand over to my shoulder and pats me awkwardly, not being one for hugs or affection. "Don't destroy yourself so quickly."

"I'll be fine, Alex." I say, although I can't tell if I'm lying or not. "I'll be fine."

"Allun started drinking again."

I inhale a deep puff and exhale slowly. Smoke rolls from my mouth, into the air, and fades into what seems to be oblivion.

Alex scratches at his neck and coughs, his eyes turning watery. I don't know the source of it, but I scoot away so I don't catch anything. "He, uh... He's had a rough time. Won't even talk to Taius. I had to do all the talking, and I'll have to relay it to Taius."

"Why won't he talk to Taius?" I ask curiously.

He goes quiet and pale, obviously not knowing how to phrase what he's going to say next. He sighs. "He blames Taius for the death of his youngest son," He stares into my eyes, unblinking. "Walder."

I close my eyes and take a deep breath. I almost forgot about that son of a bitch. Hell, I forgot I was living in his old penthouse suite. I want to spit at the sound of Walder's name. If Walder is Allun's son, I certainly hope father and son are very different in this instance. That rape-loving, blood-hungry coward was a blight on the face of existence. It was well-deserved, what I did to him. Should there be a Hell, may he rot in its most horrifying and twisted layer.

"Does he know I did it?" I ask the only thing I can think up at this point.

He shakes his head, frowning. "No, and I suggest we do not tell him. God knows what he might do."

3

Alex

"I know we need to help the family, but I don't know if we can spare Praxis."

Taius stands in his penthouse, looking out through the big, open window into the dark void of space.

Stars are strewn all throughout the galaxy, each one taking its respective place. Despite that we know all about them, I still like to think there's some mystery to stars; there might still be something about them we haven't been able to figure out. That most likely isn't the case, sadly, but I like to think that it is.

Taius glances over his old war medals, which are mounted on the wall beside him. He examines them carefully, keeping his gaze locked on the image of himself just beside them. The picture depicts him, youthful and smiling, while riding down a dirt road with a group of fellow soldiers in a foreign territory.

The image seems pleasant, if you don't know the story behind it. He was young--too young to see the horrors of war, in my opinion. The truck they were in stopped. There was a loud screaming. The journalist who took the picture hopped off the back and took off running, leaving Taius and the platoon behind. The driver jumped out. Taius, of course, realized something was up. He fled out the back, leading the group onward.

As he was trying to pull a few out, there was an explosion. He fell back; convoy trucks started exploding, and good men he knew were dying. This was before he even reached the base he was going to settle at.

"Why can't we spare her? The family needs help and we have plenty of guards hanging around the station. Not to mention the hit-men." I reply, but Taius just shakes his head. His gaze slowly breaks from the photograph and turns to me, his glowing eyes faded with age and past drug-use. He sighs and sits himself down on a stool at his personal bar. I sit down beside him and look to him, seeking any sort of answer. Finally, he speaks up again.

"Praxis is the law. Without Praxis, we revert to anarchy. You think the guards won't like a chance to abuse their authority again?" Taius says, but it only brings forth further questions from me.

I reach into my coat pocket and pull forth a bottle of water, sipping from it before continuing this conversation. "*You* be the law, then, Taius." I urge him, but he dismisses it.

"I am not the law-maker. I have my own troubles. We need Praxis." He says sternly, as if he were lecturing me.

"Funny. You were really opposed to making her justicar when I asked you to before." I remind him of his previous opposition to the idea. I remember my dear older brother's words when I first brought it up: 'fuck no.'

"You were asking me to put a girl--not a woman, a *girl*--in charge of an entire justice system." He defends his previous point, although it has long since been proven wrong. I give him a shrug and shake my head, seeing as I wasn't quite sure of putting her in charge myself, at the time.

That being said, Walder wanted anarchy. He wanted rape, murder, theft, he wanted all of this horrible shit. I needed to figure out a replacement for him; I needed to find someone I could trust. An associate of the Vortigan family wasn't--and isn't--exactly trustworthy, and God knows any good men for keeping the peace in the family are long dead or unwilling.

"The last guy we had in charge was a boy--not a man, a *boy!*" I allude to Walder, a balls-out, gun-toting, dick-in-hand, slave-raping psychopath. Walder was a pedophile, a rapist, a murderer, an anarchist, a bum--more than all of that, though, he was pathetic. The product of childhood neglect through his father's struggle with depression. He had no proper raising, developed no sense of empathy; he was a cold son of a bitch. I mean that literally, by the way: son of a bitch. I fucking hate his mother. No idea why Allun ever married her. "And the last time I checked, he wasn't handling justice very well, himself."

"Look, you proved me wrong. Is that what you wanna hear, Alex?" Taius asks me bitterly.

I shake my head and wave my hands over one another to signal a 'no.' "I want to hear 'yes.' I want to hear 'Praxis can go with you to Sar Vort, Alex. Thanks for being such a good brother. You mean a lot to me.'"

"Kiss my ass." Taius says with a serious look on his face, but it soon breaks into a smile. "Alright, fine. Praxis can go with you to Sar Vort. Please, for the love of god, don't get her killed. I don't know who we'd appoint if she died."

"It's set, then?" I ask before I order a ship to ready itself for us.

Taius nods, but halts me with one hand before I call any of the pilots on the dock. "What is it?"

"There's a guy--a prisoner, actually—who I want you to take out before you leave. "Taius requests.

"What'd he do?"

"Hell if I know. Praxis recommended it."

* * * *

The prison of Proscriptus is small and makeshift. Mostly because we weren't originally supposed to have a prison. Changes come and changes go, though.

It's colder than a Northern Undrian's balls in here, but it does its job. My boots make loud thuds as I walk into the prison room, eyeing prisoners along the way. A guard with a cold gaze and a stone heart almost Vortigan guards have--guides me into the prison. Convicts glare on, but they know better than to say anything. Say anything to Vortigan--even an adopted one--that's out of order, and you'll find yourself floating through space without a suit.

"The man you're after in here is a former Dreadwal soldier. They may not be too happy if they find out he's dead." The guard speaks cautiously.

"Is it your fucking job to give me advice?" I bark in reply.

What the hell was our recruiter thinking hiring someone that speaks out of line? It ain't like I'm going to kill him, but I'm sure as shit not happy about having him in our Warden Division if he's going to make slips of the tongue like this. The guard tries not to look nervous as he stops by the cell, but I can smell the worry on him. He stands still in front of me, but I can see his rifle shaking in his hands.

"Sorry, sir." He says, his voice getting shaky.

I take a deep breath. "You know, looking shaky, even sounding shaky, it ain't good for a warden. If I were a prisoner, I'd stab you in the fucking neck if I saw you shaking like you are. Man up, asshole." I punch him in the gut and rip the key card from his back pocket when he doubles over, swiping it and opening the cell door. "You may think I'm being a dick. Maybe I am, but it's for your benefit, kid."

I glance into the cell and see the prisoner sitting on his metal bed, looking out his unbreakable window into the void. He's trying to pretend he doesn't see me coming.

"You." I gain his attention, sliding my blaster-pistol out of its holster. "You hear about what happened in Sar Vort?" I ask, taking initiative for myself. Allun mentioned that he suspects it might be one of the other families. A Dreadwal soldier, even a former one, might have some insight.

"I don't hear about much in this shitty little cell." He eyes me over. He might have a plan to attack me.

I hold out my pistol to his face, showing him that I'm not afraid to kill his ass. A Tartuan soldier of any sort always has a plan to kill everyone they meet. You've got to be careful if you're interrogating them. "So, uh. What happened?"

"A Vortigan plant was bombed a few days ago." I answer and spit in disgust when I see a smile grown on his face.

He goes to open his mouth, but I already know he doesn't know anything. I can read it in his expression. I blast a shot into his chest. He screams before I expelled one into his head. He falls back against the wall, slides down the back wall, off of the bed and onto the floor with a thud. I turn and see the guard, still holding his stomach from where I punched him.

"... Y-... You killed him outright. W-with a blaster." The guard mutters, shocked and slightly mortified.

"Kid, how did you become a Vortigan soldier?" I ask, honestly surprised at the absolute level of innocence that seems to be in this kid's face now that he's seen an execution.

"I'm not really a soldier yet, sir... M-more of a recruit..." He stutters too much. I sigh.

"Well, kid. Get used to this shit."

* * * *

"Praxis." I say as I step aboard the ship, lighting myself a smoke. "Be prepared for Tartarus."

4

Allun

It's been quite a while since I've seen Alex. I've been told that he's really aged a lot. It's sad, having an adopted Alkin brother. It's sad because it's like owning a pet. Not to dehumanize Alex, of course, but the fact is that he does not have the lifespan of a Tartuan. We live for such a long time that the time spent with my little brother is going to be very short.

It saddens me, though. I love my little brother more than anything. I love my whole family more than anything, to the point that they mean the world to me. I may have shunned Taius for the death of my boy. I may tell the bastard he's shit. I may spit when I hear his name. The simple fact, though, is that I act this way because I am disappointed.

My disappointment lies in the fact that, as much as I want to, I cannot hate my brother. I cannot hate anyone in my family. I cannot speak ill of my son, no matter his horrible actions, and I cannot bring myself to raise arms against my brother. If it were anyone bearing a different name that shot my boy, I would put a bullet in his skull. Not a blast from a blaster-pistol, either. A *bullet*. The difference isn't just physical, but cultural. Emotional. 'A blaster means business, a bullet means war.' That's what Ma always told me.

I sit at the docks of Sar Vort and tap my feet, reading through a book about the lives of soldiers in the Industrial Empire. I know I shouldn't be reading this, but I can't help myself. Every time I think about my two oldest boys, I have to try to remind myself that they didn't die in foreign or uncomfortable conditions. I have to know that they didn't die in a world beyond their comprehension, scared and confused. This book, sadly, doesn't make it sound too pleasant. Especially not the world they were on.

I can still remember the boys' enthusiasm. Both of them were smiling when they shipped off. 'We're gonna make the Empire proud, dad.' Why the Empire? Why couldn't they make *me* proud? The Empire doesn't give a shit about them as individuals.

Barius was sent home in pieces. Those pieces were laid out in the cryo-casket and preserved for all eternity, buried in the Vortigan family tomb. A parent should never live to see their child die, but when that child marches off for war... I would give my own life if it would bring back either one of theirs, or even Walder's.

Barius and Noris were good kids. They didn't deserve the terrible end they met. I remember Noris' corpse being sent back shortly after Barius' surviving pieces. His corpse was whole, at least, but missing the glow in his eyes. They said it was a jungle disease that got to him. He didn't even die in service of the Empire, like he'd have wanted, if he was to die.

I snap out of my train of melancholy reminiscence. I lay down the book and try not to weep for my boys. I watch the ports carefully. Ships come and go, landing, unloading and leaving as quickly as they came. They disappear into the smoggy sky, some to return and others never to be seen on Tartarus again. I keep an eye out for any Alkin, seeing as my little brother is Alkin himself. I haven't seen Alex in a very long time and really can't wait to see him again. I was just relieved when I found out he didn't die on Alkineth, with that massive war that happened.

The gray and depressing scene of the docks slowly fades from my thoughts as I examine a large carrier ship that appears to be landing. It lands with a light *clink* against the ground and slowly slides its doors open. A large cluster of slaves walk off, being marched on by armed guards.

The scaly, beaked Astarian slaves drag themselves sadly out of the ship and off of the docks, into a caged slave-truck waiting just beyond the port. Squawks, clicks and chirps of despair all echo. The creatures don't even have their speech collars, so no one understands a damn thing that they're saying. It's probably better that way.

Slaves may have thoughts and feelings. They may be people, but it's better for our society to pretend that they aren't. One of the guards lets off a shot near the cage to scare them, causing them all to screech and push back against the cage. Two of the guards climb into the cab of the truck and pull off, disappearing around the corner, probably headed to an auction house.

I turn my attention back to the docks and see, finally, the two Alkin I was on the lookout for. Alex is a withered-looking old man now, and I can't help but consider again the fact that he'll probably be dead soon. I see his beard and feel somewhat envious. Tartuans are rarely able to grow facial hair, but here's this old bastard with a full goatee. I rush forward to hug him, hoisting him in the air like a child. I give him a kiss on the cheek and a grin, patting him on the shoulder even when I let him back down. "Alex, you old bastard! Welcome home!"

"Thanks, Allun. It's good to see you again." He smiles wearily, probably tired from the journey. He always had a hard time sleeping in ships. "This is Taius' branch's Justicar, Praxis. Praxis, Allun."

I turn my attention to a beautiful young woman in a black business suit and a skirt, with perfectly straight, thick black hair and bright yellow eyes. I glance over her and notice three blaster-pistols held away in different spots, two at the hips, one in the suit jacket's inside pocket. She's prepared, but she needs to keep them hidden better. She doesn't smile or really show any expression. She shakes my hand and steps back into her place. I like the fact that she seems all-business.

"Nice to meet you, Praxis." I say, smiling in company of family. Had I met her without Alex being present, I'd probably have her same demeanor. She nods and takes an attentive stance, her hands at her front and her eyes going between Alex and me, but paying enough mind to the world around her. "So, you two have anywhere to stay?"

"I figured we'd just stay with Ma." Alex says with uncertainty, scratching his neck. He's already broken sweat in the heat of the Industrial Homeland. Our whole world is like one giant, sweaty, unforgiving factory.

I shake my head and grin, happy to have my brother back home.

"Nonsense! She's already got Orvia staying, probably going to bring Iria back home too. You can stay with me. We've got plenty of room."

I think about the available rooms. We used to have one guest room, but with the loss of my boys, now we've got three. Walder's old bedroom wasn't getting any use even before his death, so it got converted to a study.

God, I wish I hadn't done that. If only I'd known he would die so young...

I seem cursed. I consider myself cursed, and I ain't even a superstitious man. Alex smiles and nods, but I can already see the disdain for my wife in his eyes. "Eh, don't worry about Rin, she ain't saying much lately." Rin is my wife, although I'm not sure for how much longer.

* * * *

"Rin, I brought Alex and the justicar! Set out some extra plates for dinner!" I say as I enter through the front door, Praxis and Alex following closely behind me, glancing around the house.

My hunting trophies are all lined across the walls, suits of other family patriarchs and matriarchs I've brought down set up on mannequins, each one with its respective owner's family crest on a patch over the heart. I can't wait for the next one. It's going to be the Dreadwals. I have a damned good feeling it's going to be the Dreadwals.

"I'm not making dinner!" Rin yells back defensively, as if I were planning on it.

I sigh and shake my head, glancing back at Alex and Praxis and smiling as if everything were okay.

"I didn't say you were! I just asked you to set up the plates!" I yell back.

I can hear her huff all the way from the kitchen. She storms out of the kitchen and glares at Alex and me, trying not to grit her teeth. "Don't expect me to do everything for you, asshole." She growls. "Take those plates and shove 'em up your ass!"

"Love you too, dear." I groan sarcastically and lead my guests into the kitchen.

I went with a quaint kitchen when having my house built, unlike Ma. She has a team of chefs in her home, which bothers me quite a bit. Why the hell would you *need* a team of chefs in the first place?

I open up the long, flat fridge that lays out across the ground and glance about it, but find that we lack any leftovers. I start to move to the pantry. "So what do you guys want in terms of food?"

"Uh, how about we go out?" Alex suggests hesitantly, while Praxis continues to keep quiet.

I consider it. If I do make food, Rin will get pissed off and bitch at me for wasting our food despite the fact that it will be serving its purpose. I nod and grab a hat from the rack by the kitchen door, that I left there earlier today. "I know this great little place, Mr. Arigor's, you'll love it. You ever have genuine Tartuan food, Praxis?"

"No sir." She states quickly and coldly.

I grin, pleased with her demeanor. "You'll love it."

* * * *

"This food is great!" Alex announces after swallowing his first mouthful, staring back at the nervous chefs who are anxiously awaiting reply.

They all sigh a breath of relief and smile at each other, pleased with their work only for the fact that Alex was pleased with it. You *always* want to make sure the Vortigans are pleased, no matter who you are or where in space. It can be very lucrative.

I toss the head chef a three-hundred Industria coin, to split between the three chefs. He thanks me, kisses my hand and returns to his fellow chefs, ordering them back into the kitchens. I stare down at my bowl. Noodles, rakia meat, a sprinkle of werio--a native Tartuan spice--as well as leaves of a trcc that I don't recognize.

The restaurant smells far better than most places on Tartarus, smelling of cooked meats and spiced wine while sounds of laughter and the words of couples at different tables echo around us. The rest of Tartarus, while industrious and covered in beautiful architecture, smells of smoke and burning fossil fuels and sounds of gears, yelling, crying and the squawking Astarian slaves. Damned be the squawking of slaves. I use slaves, I do, but I acknowledge them as people. It's still not too lucky for them though, because I don't like people.

A bright light hangs over each table, but the spaces between tables are dark. I can see the very youthful face of Praxis, examining everything around us. She eyes the steak knife in her hands and scratches it against the napkin. The napkin tears and she seems pleased. She knows that, if she needs to, she can either kill or seriously injure someone with this knife relatively easily. Alex and I begin discussing our youth, when we would sneak out and go into the scrapyard through a hole in the fence, fight with the other boys and girls in there, make some money, gamble it away with even more of the other boys and girls... Good times.

Praxis interrupts us hastily."Business." She states bluntly. "I don't want to interrupt your reminiscence, but I didn't come here to hear about your childhoods. I came here to find out who's been slaughtering our guys and put a bullet in his head. If I don't do that, what the fuck did you bring me for?"

I want to be offended, and I am, but I can't bring myself to say anything. She's assertive; that's very admirable in a justicar. "Right." I say, sliding out of my happy, false skin of a mood. I take a deep breath and sigh, thinking back on the body count. A lot of good people died. "A compound was bombed, and I've heard talk of bombing several more. I don't know if every claim is legitimate, but we need to find the mastermind and put a stop to it--or at least find someone important enough to put a halt to their operation for a while."

"What do we know?" She asks, my gaze locked on her yellow eyes.

I think back on the details. I found a rat a while back, but he didn't tell me the damned family name. He only told me it was one of the other families we have ties with. Wouldn't answer further and we'd already tortured him to his breaking point, so I shot him in the head and dropped him off in an alley. I can only hope that his employers found him and realized that they were fucked.

"Another family." I tell her, but I honestly can't say much more.

She looks displeased, but tries not to show it too much. I can see through her guise of patience.

"We don't know who, except that we have close ties with 'em. I was thinking Tennuses or Dreadwals."

"So, no other information?" She says with what almost sounds like bitterness.

I sigh and shake my head, giving her a sympathetic, dull half-smile. "There's a Tennus soldier by the name of Carius that hangs around the Ripi's Nest pub every so often. I've talked with him before, but he doesn't exactly seem smart. Still, he might give a lead. Talks like he's hot shit--some kinda war hero, or something." I say, recounting from personal experience. The Ripi's Nest is exactly where I think I'm going tonight after I drop these two off back at my home. Get a drink."
maybe some other services. "I'd suggest hanging out there tomorrow. He comes in, question him."

"I'm guessing this isn't a high-end place?" She says. I smile and laugh.

"Nope. People tend to get kinda handsy there, too." I look around for a moment to check for anyone who may be listening. It doesn't appear that there are any spies in the area. Not that this seems to be the part that would draw attention, of course. "Anyone grabs you, tell 'em no. They keep on, show them your badge. They keep going, do what you will."

"If there's a family war coming on, a lot of people will die." Alex says, looking to Praxis first and then to me.

I nod. "It's gonna be fun."

* * * *

"Allun!" I hear the bartender greet me loudly as I enter the dingy little pub.

A neon sign out front with native Tartuan written across it blinks brightly, even through the window, but the letters for the R and P in 'Ripi' are fried. "What can I get for my favorite Vortigan?"

I glance over an Astarian slave, who wipes down a table before moving past two other slaves. A young-adult Space-Born boy, with the glowing eyes of a Tartuan and the body and hair of an Alkin. Poor bastard didn't choose his birth, but they're slaves by right of race. Same for a girl, but with more of a volumized Tartuan hairstyle as opposed to the boy's Alkin.

"Get me somethin' stiff, Jerus." I sit down and look over to the slaves, considering service from either of them. I decide against it, knowing that they've got enough to deal with as Space-Born, slaves and prostitutes all at once that they shouldn't have to worry about pleasing an aging, depressed Tartuan.

Jerus smacks his Astarian slave across the face. It squawks, the collar translates an apology for whatever the poor thing did, and it brings me the drink Jerus pours.

"Thank you." I say to Jerus, but wink so that the Astarian knows I was thanking it as well.

It lets out a pleased coo. I can never tell the difference between the sexes on Astarians, but it doesn't really matter. Not like anybody's fucking them in the first place. I keep my gaze on everything but the drink itself. For some reason, I don't want to look directly at it.

I lock eyes with a boy across the room. He's young, but mature; damn, he's pretty. I wave him over, and he looks almost flattered that I'm calling him to me. "A-Allun Vortigan..." He says quietly, his soft-looking lips moving gently, his mouth barely letting a voice slip through as he speaks. He seems almost impressed by my presence in a shitty little place like this. "It's an honor."

"What's your name, kid?" I ask, pulling a cigar from a box inside my coat pocket and lighting it up. It's a no-smoking joint, seeing as Jerus is allergic, but it ain't like he can say much to *me* about it. He knows Vortigans pretty well. We get what we want. Jerus is the type of guy that, if you have enough power, he'll let you fuck his wife. Hell, he might let you fuck his daughter. He's a pushover; he abuses his slaves and overall I don't particularly like him, but he serves me my drinks. That's his job, and when it comes to professionals, I judge people by the way they do their jobs. So I guess Jerus is an okay guy, by that standard.

"T-Tirus. Tirus Corigus." He says nervously, on the verge of blushing.

"Well, Tirus... What say you and I get a little privacy in the back?"

The boy stands, his long hair flowing down past his shoulders.

I smirk and stand up with him, putting my arm around his waist and pulling him close. I might actually keep in touch with this boy. Not often you see one quite this pretty. "Jerus, I'm going into the back! Anyone back there?"

"Better not be!" Jerus barks back in jest, but nobody laughs but him.

I walk Tirus down a musty old hall to the back, press open the door to Jerus' guest room and cop a feel of Tirus' ass. *This would piss off my wife so bad.*

5

Praxis

The Ripi's Nest, as I predicted, is not high-end. It's a dusty, sleazy little dive with a staff of four waiters, a bartender and three slaves.

It didn't seem very busy earlier in the day, but it seems that now it's getting busier. Gangs from off of the street, Vortigan soldiers, Tennus and Dreadwal soldiers, and of course some individuals. There are several Tartuans, but there seem to be two Delkyrians having a drink together and an Undrian that, as it appears, guards the door when things get busy. *Add one to the staff*, I say to my mental checklist. I have to keep tabs on everything.

I notice a Tartuan man staring at me from across the room, smirking a bit. He's wearing Tennus armor, so he might know who I'm looking for.

I stand, unbutton my shirt a little to reveal some cleavage, and approach. Sometimes sex appeal can bring more people to talk than torture and interrogation. I take a seat on the stool beside him and look at him as if he were the only attractive man in the bar. His smirk turns to a grin, pleased with himself.

The Tennus soldier waves the bartender over, "Get me a Barius Anticus and..." He pauses and looks to me, "Can I buy you a drink?"

"I'll have the Barius Anticus as well." I tell the bartender, though the soldier feels the need to repeat me. I suppose that's what he thinks passes for assertive, making himself feel like he's thinking for someone else.

"So, what brings an Alkin to Sar Vort?" He asks me, his gaze obviously moving down to my cleavage.

The men here are so blatant, lacking any sort of tact; I suppose that can be brought on from the fact that they're used to Tartuan women who, in my experiences with Tartuan culture, are very much the same way. My gaze moves off of him for just a moment as I see the Space-Born slave girl grabbed by the wrist and dragged into the back hall, the Vortigan soldier who does it leaving an Industria coin in a little box on the wall. The poor girl looks pitiful. I'd like to help her, but that isn't my job.

I turn back to the Tennus soldier. "Just exploring." I say innocently enough, as the bartender brings us our drinks. I gaze at the tall glass of a very gray looking liquid. *Oh hell, if the Tartuans drink it...* I sip it. It's actually not that bad. A little sour, but not disgusting. "What brings the Tennus family to Sar Vort?"

"I mean, our platoon's leader asked for passage into the city is all." He says nervously. "So, do you know why they call it a Barius Anticus?" He changes the subject, but it would be suspicious if I just cut back to it. I'll humor him for a moment. "The drink's name was coined just a few hundred years ago. There was a big war with the Tecorian family and all the other family on Tartarus. The Tecorians were getting bigger, stronger, started taking cities from other families with this idea that they should own Tartarus. Well, there was this boy, Barius Anticus, who had just joined the ranks of the Dreadwal family. The boy was just barely an adult, home burned down when his father fired shots back at the Tecorians."

"Sounds like his father was a brave man." I say, feigning interest. I know the damn story. Taius fought in the war.

"Yeah, but this isn't about his father. This boy escaped the fire and was absolutely pissed. Joined the Dreadwals, took up arms, killed and cut the ears off every Tecorian soldier he met. He was bitter, but he was good, just like the drink. They named the drink after him not because he was a soldier, because he was a hero. He piloted his ship--deliberately, to save everyone in a big, big battle--right into Tecorian Tower. Killed every member of the Tecorian family in there. Thing is, though, it didn't kill him. He and the surviving men on his little carrier got out and shot down every Tecorian they could find before they were finally overcome."

"Wow, you know a lot about the war..." I feign idiocy, this time, pretending to be impressed. Everyone knows about the war. Just about every Tartuan soldier who was born before that period fought in the damn war.

"Well I was in it!" He grins smugly.

I want to bash his head in every time I see that smile. I run my hand down the chest-plate of his armor and pull it away just before I reach his groin.

"Say, did you ever meet anyone named Carius?" I inquire.

He groans and leans back in his seat. "Carius, Carius; everyone always wants Carius! I led the fucking charge, all he did was give the order. *Oh, Captain Carius! Captain Carius!* All I ever fucking hear. You want Carius, he's the one with the bird on his chest."

The soldier points me in the direction of a large round table in the corner, where Carius sits with one other soldier and drinks. He does, in fact, have a large bird painted across the chest of his armor. Very crudely painted, as well; it was possibly even done by him. The rest of his armor is normal, though. Black chest-plate, black leg-pieces, yellow stripes down the sides from the shoulders to the boots.

I approach the drunken, smiling man and his soldier friend. He's not bad looking, nor is his friend. If only I had some free time. "Carius?" I ask softly, leaning over.

He looks down my shirt bluntly, just like every other soldier in this bar has since I unbuttoned this damned shirt.

"I heard *you* led the charge." I say vaguely.

What charge, I don't know, but he's not going to pass up a whore-mongering opportunity. He smiles and looks to his friend, who nods in approval.

"You wanna... Get a room in the back?"

"... Can my friend here come?" He asks. I was hoping to get him alone. Two people and I might have to kill his friend, but I suppose saying yes is the best way to win him over. If I have to kill his friend, so be it.

"Sure." I smile and lead them to the back.

They both smack me on the ass as I walk. They drop money in the box for the rented room, and I pick the room. I guide them through an open door into a dim but wide room with a big bed in the middle and a TV hanging on the wall across from it.

The door closes behind us and Carius leans in to kiss me. He pushes me down onto the bed and pins my wrists, while his friend stands awkwardly behind him.

When he releases my wrists, I reach down and pull a small holdout blaster from its hidden position on my hip. I release a suppressed shot into the wall, not making more than a sizzling noise but leaving a decently sized burn mark, and press the hot gun to Carius' forehead. He whimpers, suddenly realizing his position. As his friend goes for his gun, I fire in his direction. The white, crackling blast zips by his head and lights up the room for a moment before burning the door. I reach down for my badge with the other hand, but Carius knocks the gun from my hand and tries to pin my wrists again.

"Praxis, Vortigan Justicar." I state, glaring at him.

He doesn't seem to notice, smacking me across the face and leaning in to kiss me, more aggressively this time. The fear that was on his face disappears and is replaced with anger. I don't feel bad in the slightest for this would-be rapist piece of shit. I headbutt him in the nose, causing him enough pain to force a release. I grab him by the neck and begin to choke him, still staring at his friend.

His accomplice rushes for his gun, his hand sliding down his hip.

I release Carius and move toward the companion. I drive my fist to his throat, causing him to choke. He falls over, wailing in agony and gasping for breath. I pull the gun from his hip as he flails and fire into his head. I can hear panic in the main room of the bar. The shot echoes through the narrow halls and into the ears of the patrons. The friend is dead.

I aim for Carius, who attempts to draw his own blaster now. I shoot him in the hand, burning off three of his fingers and searing a good portion of the hand itself.

"Now you're going to tell me what the hell Tennus soldiers are doing in Sar Vort and how it may relate to the bombings. Got it?" I fire at the bed beside him.

He screeches and clutches his burned hand, making an effort to try and scoop up the severed fingers as if he could do anything to salvage them.

"Go to hell, you crazy bitch!" He screeches and picks himself up, charging at me like an angry bull. He wails when I let off another shot and step out of the way, kneecapping him. He collapses by the doorway, screaming for help. I pull my badge, flashing it as the door opens. Several Tennus soldiers stare on in shock as their captain screams. "What are you bastards waiting for? Kill her!"

"Do it and you start a war between families. Your whole platoon gets executed. Any Tennus ambassadors in the city will be executed along with you. Do you understand?" I bark, my gun turned for them.

They nod, staring on with empathy for their wounded and crying Captain Carius.

"Now go."

They disband after a moment of gawking at the situation.

I press the gun to Carius' forehead, glaring into his eyes. "What the hell business does the Tennus family have in Sar Vort?" I lower the gun, tucking it away in the back of my pants, and grab his free hand. I crack one finger and he screeches even more.

"The Dreadwals! It was the Dreadwals! They planted the bomb!" He yelps in agony and I crack another finger. "M-My platoon assisted! We were going to help them shoot up another Vortigan location!" And there goes the third. "That's all I know! Look, m-my platoon doesn't act for the whole family! Please! Don't start killing my men! Please!"

I pull the gun again and blast him in the head. His fried skull stares back at me, one eye burned and the other fading. I step out and shake my head, watching the bar's business flee.

"What the fuck is wrong with you?" The bartender growls. "Vortigan or not, you scared away my business! What the hell?"

I shoot a bottle on his shelf. It shatters, glass flying about the bar. An Astarian slave watches me go in awe and horror simultaneously. "Next time you talk to me like that, it won't be a bottle. That will be your head."

* * * *

"The Dreadwals!" Allun punches the wall of a warehouse he told me to meet him in after I got the information.

Several Vortigan soldiers stand around us, their black uniforms creased, flat and straight. They each hold their rifles close to their chests, keeping attention on Allun. The washed-up older Tartuan looks like he's going to give himself a heart attack, bloodying his knuckles against the wall.

"Those bastards! Those horrible fucks! I'm gonna kill every fucking one of those rakia-blowing pricks!" He turns to me, smiling a malicious grin and yanking a cigarette from his coat pocket and setting its head ablaze with an oil lighter. He brushes his hand through his short, curly black hair and grins, showing slightly yellowed teeth. "We're gonna teach those fuckers a lesson."

"What do you anticipate?" I ask him, almost pleased by the thought of shooting some of those arrogant Dreadwal fuckers. I've met a few of them before. I can't wait to drop some of those Dreadwal family heads into the fucking fire.

"I say we go find one of the Dreadwal brothers who are in the city and make him take a short step off a tall building." Allun is much more pleased than I am, I'd say, but he has more of a history with them. The Vortigans and the Dreadwals, despite their alliance and their ambassadors and what have you, have been at each others throats for ages. They hated each other long before I was alive and no doubt will hate each other long after I'm dead. That is to say, unless one wipes out the other sometime soon. "I still can't believe I was right. Come on."

"We're going? Right now?" I ask, a bit surprised that he'd just rush to it. In my experience, going after important figures takes a lot more planning. "Shouldn't we prepare?"

"You got a gun on you?" He asks, not even looking in my general direction. He rushes out the door, three soldiers following behind him. He glances back and I nod. "Then we're prepared. Come on." I follow him beyond the tall white walls of the empty warehouse and into the straight black length of the Tartuan equivalent of a limo.

We leave the hot, sweaty atmosphere of Tartarus and feel almost isolated within the cool, breathable air of the car. Blue lights line the ceiling of the car, giving everything a dramatic glow. "Who's the youngest Dreadwal brother?"

"Teris." I inform him, having met Teris before. I hated the little bastard more than anything. Just a teenager, but he thinks he's tough. Killing him isn't going to be that difficult. Doesn't even like having guards around him. Only keeps one with him when he goes out, even here in Sar Vort. God knows there isn't a soul that wouldn't want to kill him in this city. "Where does Teris Dreadwal usually hang out?"

"I dunno." He thinks for a moment and then turns to one of the soldiers. "Call Alex, tell him I want a meeting set up with Teris Dreadwal at the hotel on Sixth, penthouse room nine-twenty-two."

* * * *

"So what's your take on all this?" Allun asks me before taking a heavy gulp from his flask. He takes a deep breath, having a hard time breathing likely due to all of the smoke he's constantly inhaling. He stares at me, awaiting an answer.

I shrug and don't say anything.

"No, no, no. You've been all business since you got here. You've been looking at the entire situation objectively. I wanna know your opinion now."

"Honestly... I don't think I have one." I answer, having a revelation about myself. I don't recall ever really thinking about the situation beyond what to do and who to kill. I never really thought about who I'm killing or who I'm killing for, nor have I considered *what* I'm killing for. What cause could I really be furthering? I find that it's best not to think about who I'm killing or what for, because then I might sit on the fence. Sitting on the fence can be dangerous, especially in this business.

"Everybody's got an opinion." Allun tries to correct me.

I shake my head, keeping cold, emotionless eye contact. I don't want him to think I'm looking too deep into this. The only thing almost as bad as a rat to a Vortigan family head is an indecisive soldier.

Allun shrugs. "Well aren't you just a killing machine." He says sarcastically, turning to the door. The car slows to a stop. "Come on, we've got some balls to bust." He steps out of the car, straightening his shirt and pants, checking the pistol in his jacket pocket. "Is it sticking out?" He asks me.

I examine it. Seems flat. "No." I tell him and we enter the hotel, our three soldiers walking in behind us. Allun turns to them and instructs two to wait on the fire escape, while another joins us. Allun pats me down to check for my guns and finds that I have one tucked away in the back and one in my coat pocket. He decides that I'm packed well enough and we head up the elevator.

I eye the soldier behind us. Strong-jawed, muscular but not ripped, beautiful hair... He's pretty. I smile at him when Allun is looking away and he smiles back.

I turn back to the elevator door. It slides open on the top floor--floor nine--and Allun leads us out into the open hallway. We approach room twenty-two and Allun doesn't bother knocking.

He slides a badge over the scan-lock that allows him access, pulls his gun and slides the door open quickly, immediately taking note of an armed guard standing at the front. He blasts the guard in the face, scorching it beyond recognition. The guard dies from the immense pain it causes, leaving his face as a smoking crater.

I enter the room quickly, as well as the soldier, the three of us all looking for traces of the Teris. The boy quickly hops up from behind the counter and fires a few shots in our direction. I fire back once, burning a hole in his right shin.

I blast him in the hand, and Allun rushes toward him, grabbing him by the collar. "Open up the balcony door." I tell the soldier and he obliges.

I glare at Teris as Allun pulls the boy up by his shirt collar. I examine the boy before he will inevitably die. I get a sense for the kind of person he was through his tattoos and his jewelry. He has a tattoo across his neck--near his collarbone--that says 'Die Humans', written in English so that a good portion of humans will understand it. His black hair is shaved off to nothing but a fuzz and he wears a black button-down and dress pants, with an Astarian-head necklace draped around his neck.

"Teris Dreadwal." I state, approaching him.

Allun punches the boy across the face, loosening a tooth. It's hanging out, bending over the gum. Allun punches him again, and the tooth comes out, hitting the floor with a click that's followed by a yelp from Teris.

The boy shakes, cries and flails. It's obvious he's never felt real pain, because I'm sure if a punch like that had been delivered to Allun he'd have struck back. The boy tries to punch Allun in the gut with his good hand, but only manages to get it broken when I step in. He screams as his hand goes limp, dangling uselessly.

"What do you know about the bombing?"

"What the fuck are you talking about, you crazy bitch?" He screams, spitting blood as he yells it.

Allun delivers another punch to his cheek and I can already see bruises under his eyes, although he's not going to live long enough for them to hurt him in the long run.

"The compound bombing, you piece of shit!" Allun retorts. Teris spits at Allun, who responds by knocking out another tooth.

Allun, blood and saliva still on his face, hoists the boy up by the collar, although he tries to drop himself back onto the floor in rebellion. "Up or I break your one good leg!"

Allun cracks him in the nose. Black tar-like blood drips from Teris' mouth, chin and nose.

The boy fearfully stands, barely able to hold himself up with his shaky legs. For an avid anti-human Tartuan supremacist, I've noted that the boy had no problem with human goods. His shirt is obviously human-made, for instance, as well as his pants.

"Yeah, look, I... I gave the order, alright?" Teris wails, the bruises around his eye swelling up quickly. Any semblance of health he may have had (although he was a drug-user, so there wasn't much) is gone with the beating Allun gave him. "I thought... Well, you Vortigan pieces of shit deserve it!"

"You little son of a bitch! You come into *my* city," Allun punches him in the stomach as hard as he can. The boy screams, and I can see bloody piss dripping down his leg. "You send a bomb truck into *my* compound," he punches again.

The tears stream down Teris' face and mix with the blood near his mouth. He gasps for air, only to be met with another organ-smashing punch. "And most of all, you piece of filth, you betray *my* fucking family? I will end your fucking life!"

"I-I'm s-s-sorry!" Teris cries, coughing more blood up onto Allun's shoes. This display of passionate violence *almost* makes me feel sorry for the boy. But, if he would so willingly throw away our men's lives and his family's relations with us because of personal grudges, he deserves it.

"Come on, Praxis, let's see if vermin can fly!" Allun rips the necklace from the boy, breaking the chain, and tosses it to me. I hide it away in my pocket, despite that it's covered in drying blood.

Allun drags him toward the open balcony doors and knocks over a tall glass table in the center. The table shatters into several shards, leaving only its iron framing. Allun holds the crying boy over the balcony, staring him in the faded but still glowing eyes. "Tell me why you did it." Allun speaks through his teeth. He is, by far, the angriest person I've ever seen.

"I... I wanted to... to..." Blood spews from his mouth, pouring down his chin and neck and onto his shirt, no doubt leaving a stain. "I just wanted to do something... important... Something to give me p-p-purpose..."

"People are dead because of you." Allun growls. "Good people. Better men than you." He wipes the blood and spit from his face, gritting his teeth.

The boy looks back at him pitifully. "You've killed your father, your mother, your brothers and your sisters. You've killed your cousins aunts, uncles, friends, associates. All for a sense of purpose. During your time here in my city, you've been the negotiator to me; who am I? I'm the guy holding a gun to your family's head. You know what you just did? You just convinced me to pull the trigger."

Allun shoves and releases, watching heartlessly as the boy falls.

He screams, his eyes fading before the drop. His lungs die mid-scream as he falls through the factory smoke cloud. There's a loud crack at the bottom and then... Silence.

Allun, the soldier and I all stand in a moment of silence, in the quiet after a storm of passion and fury. Allun inspects the blood on his knuckles and then on his shoes. He glances over the broken table and moves into the penthouse room. He looks over and sees the trail of blood stains from where we caught Teris. He looks over the corpse. He sighs and gives a saddened, weary look. "We're done here. Let's go."

6

ALLUN VORTIGAN'S JOURNAL

The following is a journal entry from Allun Vortigan, given to me after I suggested to him that perhaps a journal would help with his recovery. He claimed that, as he was writing it, he almost felt himself reliving the moments as he wrote them. As his therapist, I feel great concern for him. I'm not sure if I can even help this poor man.

It was in the late days of the Tecorian War that I made my first kills. It was in the ruins of a city called Sar Drai; it was the one and only city of the Draiken family. The Tecorians had already bombed the city, caught the surviving Draiken family heads and executed them all at once in the town square, their people watching. Everyone that survived holed up in ruined buildings or fled the city entirely to seek shelter from one of the other major families--hopefully none as batshit crazy as the Tecorians. Now, the Industrial Empire was never ruled by a single force. It never has been and probably never will be.

That being said, there was a collective. When the shit hit the fan, every family would throw in soldiers, and sometimes even family heads to serve in the Collective Industrial Military, or CIM. Of course, once the Tecorians tried their hand at conquest, the CIM got pretty pissed.

There I was, a private in a team of snipers. I was a shaky-handed little shit with a virgin trigger-finger. I'd never killed a man in my life, and I sure as shit didn't want it to start now. Ma told me I had to go since so many of my cousins and even my big brother were out there. Told me that I needed to serve to understand the family business. I didn't think she'd be right.

The day was brown and smoky, like most Tartarus days are, with very little wind. I was surrounded by heat and bitter men. It was on Fifth Avenue of Sar Drai that I was holed up in a skyscraper.

There was a bridge right across from me, probably a good sixty feet below me, where the Draiken family's bodies were hanging. It was gruesome, but I'd seen my share of bodies. My Ma was a family head, after all.

I'd seen people get executed before. Hell, the woman forced me to watch when I was just a boy, but when you're *in* the shit, it's a different story. When you're forced to kill or be killed, when you're seeing innocent people (or at least decent guilty people) get gunned down, it takes a toll on you. I looked down my scope, trying not to let my hands shake the rifle as I held it out the window.

I watched a patrol pass over the bridge, a captain and a few privates, lieutenants, God knows what other ranks... but not my mark. I could hear my team talking over the intercom, all of us wondering where our target and his truck were. I could hear bombs falling, far back, as well as see the aftermath. A building in the smoggy distance rumbled as it began to collapse, indiscriminately taking countless lives upon its collapse. Whether it be civilian, Tecorian or CIM lives, it didn't matter. Bombs and rubble, despite being inanimate, were probably the most heartless killers in the war.

A squad came up to the bridge, eventually, but not one of theirs. A firefight followed, CIM soldiers in all black blasting away at the Tecorian blues and reds. Blaster energy zipped, crackled and roared for a good thirty minutes before the fight was over. The CIM squad lost, of course, given the size of the fighting force on the bridge. I wanted to help them so bad, but I knew that I was under orders. Orders in CIM were very strict. It didn't matter if you saved all of fucking Tartarus. If you didn't do it by the book, you were fucked.

"*You know what I'm gonna do when we reach Sar Tecor?*" The voice of one of our team members ripped through the comm system, the words breaking through the wall of static that seemed to block the sound-waves.

Another voice tore its way through, struggling to speak clearly in this horrible noise.

"*What are you gonna do?*" It asked amusedly, although I couldn't really identify who said it or even where they were. Despite working in a team with these people, I'd only been in the team for a short period.

I still couldn't decipher the voices over communicators. I adjusted my earpiece, still keeping an eye out for the slave truck hauling our target; he was a slaver by the name of Perosi and a loyal follower to the Tecorians. His slaves were what was running the enemy's business back home. If we could take out him and his slave trucks, we would be set. The biggest problem, though, is that those damned trucks were everywhere. We had our men tracking them, though.

"*I'm going to find the head of the Tecorian family, I'm gonna shoot him and I'm gonna ---- --- --fe right there on his corpse.*" I was sort of pleased that I didn't hear what he said there. The static certainly cut him off at a choice moment.

Before he could say anything else, we could hear it rolling. The roar of a big slave truck sputtering past overtook our ears and we saw it. This was no pickup with a cage in the back. This was a fucking monster of a slaver vehicle. This was what most slavers wished they could get.

It growled as it moved through the outpost, but there was no sign of Perosi. Rather than him, another slaver stepped out. More than likely it was one of his men, but he certainly wasn't one of his more prominent associates. He showed his ID to the outpost guards and headed back for the truck. There was already arguing over the communication waves. "*Where's Perosi?*"

"*The bastard didn't come! Who the hell tipped him off?*"

"It doesn't matter! Blow the bridge! Blow the damn bridge!"
"What about our orders?"
"Our orders didn't say anything about this, but we're not passing up that opportunity! Shoot the fucking explosives! Blow the fucking bridge!"
"We are not blowing anything, soldier! We will leave those explosives alone until--"

I didn't think about it. I just wanted the arguments to stop. I held my breath. I kept quiet and held tight. I took steady aim at our explosives--quite subtly planted on the bottom of the bridge in the night--and let off a shot. *Zzzzzssssssssip.*

My rifle released a light hissing shot and sliced through the air. I took a deep breath and watched the consequences of my actions. The loud truck honked and roared as the bridge began to crumble. I could hear the squawking of a hundred and thirty--at least, that's all the bodies that were dug up--Astarians as the truck went down into the water.

My eyes widened even more than they already were when I saw those soldiers falling with it. Their rations, their ammo, their guns, everything that was on that bridge was now being destroyed. Soldiers caught directly in the blast had it easy. They died quickly. Like I said, though, rubble was the real monster of this war. The damaged concrete rolled over probably around fifty men, while another forty got caught in the water and couldn't make their way out, either due to broken limbs or trying to carry their buddies that had broken limbs. The water was a hateful bitch to those poor souls. Out of that whole army, fifteen survived. Fifteen exact, too. I counted.

"Who just made that son of a bitch move?"
"Fess up, shithead!"

I remained quiet. All of us remained quiet, apart from those two. I was never penalized. Nobody was punished for it. Hell, they wanted to give medals to the person who did it, but I wasn't going to take all of that attention. I halted a slave operation and wiped out an outpost with a single shot and the help of some guys who put down well-placed explosives.

It was three months later that the bad shit started happening. I was at a funeral. A doctor, who had patched me up a while back after some close-calls with a Tecorian private, had shot himself due to the pain of losing his legs to an IED. Ironic, isn't it? A man who patches people up for a living shot himself because he couldn't take the pain. I want to say the doctor was a good guy, but the fact is that I didn't know the poor son of a bitch. He patched me up and he told me a few good dirty jokes. That doesn't make him a fucking hero. But, back in those days, I lied and said that I knew him well enough to attend the funeral because it would have been rude to turn the invitation down.

They tried to talk like we were giving him the funeral he deserved, but being rolled up in a tarp and stuffed into a crate in a city he wasn't from on a world that, while it was the home-world of his race, was not his own home was most definitely *not* a proper funeral. I was lucky I didn't get put down and suffer the same funeral service as the doctor. The war... It did a lot to me. It fucked up my mind and improved my body. I got strong, mentally and physically, but it absolutely devastated me emotionally. I can't handle things anymore without breaking down and resorting to violence.

Here I am today, out of the service and still killing people left and right. I tossed that boy--a *teenage* boy--from a balcony and I felt absolutely no remorse. Do you know how that feels?

-Allun Vortigan, Therapist-Ordered Journal Entry

7

Praxis

I've got a lot to think about since the death of that boy. He was a teenage boy. A piece of shit, to be sure, but a boy. He may have gotten better; he may not have. He got no trial. He didn't get to express anything. He did it, and we killed him.

I don't want to live like this. I don't want to live in the bloodshed of Tartuan family life. I never wanted to kill anyone, and now I don't even know how many lives I've ended. Part of me wants to thank Alex, while part of me wants to hit him. He's a bastard for dragging me away from Alkineth and forcing me into a life of would-be crime; but he very well may have saved my life. I consider whether or not I want out. I do, but I don't know where I'd go. I'm not going to show up on Calypso's front door asking for her to provide shelter. I don't know what to do.

I sit in my guest room and sigh, looking over the pictures on the walls. There's a portrait of a Tartuan standing in front of a line of human riflemen, taking an aggressive stance despite being the alone and unarmed. I look at the words engraved under the portrait itself and notice its title. It was aptly named "Freedom, No Matter the Cost." I find it funny that Tartuan art always portrays humans as the villains, despite there never being a war between the United Human Empire and the Industrial Empire of Tartarus. Eventually, I get tired of staring at artwork, but I note that there isn't a TV in this room. I decide I'll go find my own entertainment.

I stand and stretch, yawning before rubbing my eyes and preparing to leave the room. I step out into the wide hallway, which has a very classical-looking and beautiful floral wallpaper. The whole house is dimly lit and full of antiques, as if it were made and decorated thirty or so Tartuan centuries ago. I can hear pleasured moans from the back room, so I can only imagine that Allun's wife is taking a slave to her bed. It's not my business anyhow and, knowing Allun, he no doubt knows that she does this. I've learned to keep my head down and not stick my nose in other people's business.

It's been three weeks since we landed here and we've already forced every Dreadwal in the city into hiding. Sewers, back alleys, warehouses--they've taken to holing up in locations like this.

I start for the door, but find myself interrupted by it opening abruptly. Alex and Allun both storm in, blasters in their hands. Allun pulls a human revolver from the back of his pants, laying it down on the counter. I immediately begin to consider why he didn't use it on Teris. The entire purpose of a regular gun, at least in this day and age, is to use it to signal war. The fact that I never saw him fire the thing once means that either he's really forgetful when in the heat of a passionate, violent assault or there's something that he's plotting.

"Allun." I say acutely, turning back to him. God, I can never get away from my work. "Why didn't you fire that gun at Teris?"

"I'm sorry?" He asks, turning back to me defensively. "What the hell are you talking about?"

"That revolver. You never fired it when we killed Teris. Not once. Why?"

"Eh..." He goes quiet for a moment, looking between Alex and me suspiciously. "I was saving it."

"The custom," I feel inclined to remind him, "Is that when you fire the first shot in a war--*especially* on the one who started it--you use an old-fashioned gun. So why didn't you shoot Teris?"

"I am not returning that little shit's corpse to his family, or any of the soldiers we've been executing. I'm not going to let this start a war." Allun says irrationally, turning away from us and facing the gun.

Alex puts his hand on Allun's shoulder sympathetically. "I know you don't want further bloodshed on our side, Allun, but it's Tartuan decency to send the boy's corpse back to the family. Do you think we can just cover up the slaughter of, what, a hundred Dreadwal soldiers and a family head?" Alex asks him reasonably, but Allun refuses to listen.

"Look, if this family gets into a war while I'm still kicking, then I'm going to have to continue living a lot longer than I'd originally hoped for!"

Allun carries himself over to me and out the door. Alex and I follow behind him, hoping he doesn't go off and do something stupid or selfish. He gets into his car and starts to pull away, but stops at the end of the driveway. He leans out of his window and stares at Alex and me with probably the saddest eyes I've seen the man give in my short time knowing him. "Both of you, get in."

Hesitantly, we do as instructed. I wasn't planning on letting him drive off alone anyway. I get in the back seat and Alex gets in the passenger's side seat in the front. Allun pulls off onto the road quickly and speeds us onward toward God knows where. "Where the hell are we going, Allun?"

"We're going to go burn down a building." Allun says coldly, "Maybe kill everyone inside."

"What building?" Alex asks, terrified. Allun shrugs.

"I don't know yet. Who's somebody we don't like?" He presses his foot harder on the pedal. I'm worried he'll crash, but I keep a cool head. "Who was that guy, used to try and pick on you when we were kids?"

"No! We're not doing that!" Alex barks furiously, pointing a finger at Allun.

Allun closes his eyes, which is a terrible idea in this instance, but opens them back up again after a moment. He pulls to the side of the road and comes to a screeching halt. We find ourselves parked in front of a massage parlor.

Allun turns off the car and takes a few deep breaths. "You're right. You're right." He begins to stream tears, his head falling onto the steering wheel. "What the fuck am I doing?" He shakes his head, burying his face in his hands. "Who the fuck am I anymore?"

"You're my brother." Alex says compassionately, patting Allun's shoulder.

Allun lifts his head, tears still pouring, as he turns to face me. "Why didn't you say anything, Praxis?" He asks me.

I shrug. "No, no, shrugs won't cut it. Why the hell didn't you say anything? You just got into a car with a hysterical alcoholic. Why did you do that?"

"It felt out of line to deny you." I state.

Allun takes another deep breath and shakes his head. "Learn to think for yourself, Praxis. You're all orders. What would you do if you didn't have guys like me and Alex here to call the shots, huh?" He begins to scold me, going out of his fit of hysteria and into a fit of irritation toward my actions (or lack thereof). "A day might come when we're not calling the shots, when you have to take matters into your own hands, big, important stuff, like the war that's now most likely coming? You're a justicar. You can't just turn to me and Alex for orders. You'll be commanding a squad; hell, you may be commanding a whole platoon."

"He's right, Praxis." Alex says, turning the attention away from Allun now and onto me. "You are going to have to learn how to run the show."

* * * *

Tonight, I dream of blue again. Blue blood, dripping from the walls once more. I stand in a room leaking blue, although it doesn't flood.

A severed head, covered in blue, lies on a table in the center of the room. *Zeph.* I find myself inclined to be fearful, but something about it makes me feel angry. Something makes me feel as if I should smash the head rather than hold it.

I rush to the center of the room and flip the table, throwing it on its side. *That bastard!* I think to myself, *That lying bastard!* Despite my feelings here, I have no understanding of why I feel this way. I rush over to the fallen head and kick it, launching it into the wall. The wall shatters and the head is partially smashed. Beyond the wall is a war zone.

It's not just any war zone, but Alkineth. It's my home city, up in flames. Blaster rounds zip between sides, Alkin and human firing upon one another. *Not again.* I begin to run toward a pharmacy, but a blaster cannon hits it before I can even get there. Glass flies everywhere.

"Get that bitch!" I hear a human soldier scream, forcing me to turn in the direction of the noise.

The soldier fires his rifle, and I soon find myself running from a group of humans. They're faster than me, though. Stronger, too. I find myself pinned. Guns are pointed at me from every direction, and the human begins to tear at my clothes.

I jolt awake, fearful, unwilling to let myself continue that awful nightmare. I lie in my bed, sweaty and burning hot, wrapped in blankets. I won't suffer through another war.

* * * *

I called a meeting a few days ago with Alex. It's been two weeks since we hit Teris, and Alex called for his body to be sent back home.

We're finally sitting down and eating out, following through with the plans we made prior. I've been thinking about what he and Allun told me. That I need to forge my own path and stop taking orders. That may require me leaving. My own path can only be attained through individualism, I've decided. We sit in a wonderful little restaurant, the same Allun took us too when we first arrived. I feel almost bad as I try to start the conversation, feeling butterflies in my stomach every time I start to try and bring it up. I stare out the window, quietly. Watching the cars pass on the dark Tartarus road. The neon glow of the sign in the window lights up the street corner.

"You know, I'm worried about the idea of war." Alex sighs. The once white-bearded old man has cut the long beard and now allows the world to see his strong jaw and a scar under his lip I didn't even know he had. "If we go to war with the Dreadwals, which is inevitable given the way you and Allun killed that boy-"

"It was mostly Allun." I interrupt.

Alex shrugs. "Whoever it was," He says passively, but accusingly. I can do brutal, horrible things, but I would never have beaten the boy as badly as Allun did. "They sure did a number on him. The kid was a piece of shit, sure, but he didn't deserve to be executed in the manner that he was. One hand shot, another broken, bruises all over him, missing teeth, fractured skull, dropped off a balcony... Shit, I wouldn't wish all that on my worst enemy."

"You're not as passionate as Allun." I remind him.

He nods and lifts his drink. A Barius Anticus. My God, that drink is popular.

"Fair enough." He gulps down some of his thick, bitter beverage and sighs.

I close my eyes, nervous. I'm finally going through with it. I'm proud of myself. I may not know what the future holds, but I know for certain that this is what I want. Maybe leaving the future open is going to be good for me. Maybe I can regain my sense of individualism. *Just maybe.*

"Alex, there's... There's something I really need to tell you and... and ask you, I suppose." I start.

Alex nods, worried for what I might say. I can see it in his eyes. He knows what I'm going to ask.

"Alex, you--and all the Vortigans, excepting Walder--have been good to me. You've treated me respectfully, you've paid me well, but-"

"But now you want to go." He groans bitterly. "You don't want to be a part of this life anymore, is that it?"

"I don't want to be in another war!" I defend my point.

He nods. "And, just as well, I want to be an individual. Make my own choices, like you said."

"That's fair." He nods. "But you can't just *go*. A war is about to start, we don't have a replacement justicar in line, and I'll be damned if I'm just letting the closest thing to a child I've ever had leave. I may never see you again!"

"I mean, I'll still come back to visit." I tell him optimistically. *If my travels will allow it.* I keep that part to myself.

He looks at me sadly and takes a deep breath."If that's really what you want," He submits, "Then I'll grant it. We'll make arrangements for a new justicar starting tomorrow. I'm thinking one of the Vortigan cousins."

"Thanks, Alex." I smile at him and feel the emotion welling up inside of me. I'd be lying if I said it wasn't hard to leave him, for all the shit he's caused me. "I... I can't tell you how much it means to me that you actually give a damn about how I feel."

"You've been like a daughter to me. I can't-" He stops mid-sentence and stares out the window. He raises up his hand slowly and takes a deep breath.

I look to where he's staring. Four men, two at either window, in trench coats and hats. Machine-blasters slide from under their coattails and they raise them to the glass.

"Get down!" Alex screams in announcement, flipping the table and yanking me down with him.

I can hear the glass shatter. I see the blaster rounds zipping by, some hitting our table and some flying past us or into other customers. The manager falls dead near our table, as well as several waiters and other customers. A couple die with their hands in each others. I can at least take solace in the fact that they didn't know they were going to die before they were already dead. Life granted them the easiest way out.

After the hail of blasts is done, I can hear chattering. I can't make out a whole lot over the sirens that roll in, but I do make out several blaster shots. The area goes quiet, all except for the sirens.

Alex and I look up. Beyond the bodies and the broken glass stand several Vortigan police officers, holstering their weapons. "Mr. Alex Vortigan?" Yells an officer into the restaurant.

"Still alive!" Alex yells in return. "Can't say the same for a lot of these people."

"Christ, what happened?"

"Hell if I know. Just came over and shot up the place!"

"We're gonna need to wheel in a lot of corpses, boys."

8

Allun

"I can't believe they hit the restaurant!" I bark, slamming my fist on the kitchen counter.

Alex has a bruise on his cheek, likely from jumping down when they started firing. I'm glad he wasn't hurt, but they just went after my little brother. That was a big fucking

mistake. The difference between me hitting Teris and the Dreadwals trying to hit Alex is that Teris called for the bombing. Alex didn't have a damn thing to do with the death of that little piece of shit.

I pull an oil lighter from my pocket and light myself a cigarette, looking over at the Vortigan Chief of Police, who stands in council alongside me, Ma, Alex, Praxis and my Aunt Kaer, who took the trip here a few days ago. Aunt Kaer looks a lot like Ma, built like a brick wall, curly black hair, walks with purpose.

"Are we forgetting that your *wife* was hit as well?" Aunt Kaer asks, obviously holding no understanding of the reality behind my marriage.

Rin was shot and critically injured, and a Dreadwal assassin made an attempt on my life. I swiped his gun and beat his face in. I still remember his teeth spilling out into the ground, blood dripping down his broken face, pressing a blaster to his kidneys and pulling the trigger, over and over, burning holes deeper and deeper until I burned a hole straight through him. Rin got blasted six times from four different directions. I saw her that night, her face burned. I was furious, but I can't say it was a fury for her sake.

The fury lies more in the fact that they were trying to hurt me and my family. Rin is no longer family. Rin is not even my wife anymore. She's a stranger in my household, and we hate one another. The most tragic thing about her possibly dying is that it didn't happen sooner. After our second son died, she started blaming me. The woman I married and loved is dead now. She died a long, long time ago. She didn't just resent me, though. She resented Walder, our youngest. That's probably why he was so fucked up. I couldn't raise him; I was working; and, of course, she refused to.

"Yeah, well, Rin isn't exactly our main focus here." I say, sparking shock and offense in my Aunt. She doesn't say much on it, though, because what I've said is true: Rin is not our main focus.

Ma leans over the counter and takes a look over at the Chief, then to Alex, to Praxis, finally to me. "I'm not going to say you didn't do the right thing by killing Teris," Ma starts, regretful for not taking a more cautious approach. At least she's not pointing the finger at me. "Since I *did* give you the revolver and tell you to kill the bomber. But," And here it is. The finger. "You should have told me it was the Dreadwals before you went and blew a hole in him."

"A-" Praxis starts a word, but steps back away, going quiet. The whole circle is staring at her now. She looks at anything but Ma, intimidated by her presence. Hell, I can't blame her. The chief does the same thing every time they meet.

"Well, speak up, darling." Ma urges her on. Praxis steps back up to the counter. "What were you going to say?"

"Allun never fired the revolver." She reminds us all.

I never fired the revolver.

I smile, looking around the circle. A look of relief hits everyone involved.

Alex puts his hand on Praxis' shoulder and pulls her in tight, giving her a side-hug. He thanks her and gives her a kiss on the forehead.

"Allun never fired the revolver!" Alex repeats, "Which means... What, Praxis?"

The attention has now turned to the girl. She doesn't even have to think about it. Rather than the nervousness she had when faced with Ma, she steps up and says it. "Which means that we can still negotiate peace. Not putting a bullet in that boy was probably the smartest thing we did when we killed him."

The focus turns back to me. Ma's expression turns saddened, knowing that the punishment will no doubt be placed on me. Alex turns to me, saddened as well, then my aunt. The chief's expression is cold, but remorseful. Hey, with any luck, they might execute me.

"I'll talk to the Dreadwals, then. Are we going to send out a message to the patriarch or the brothers?" I ask inquisitively. I have no fear for what will happen if I show up. They'll kill me, or put me in prison, or cut off my hands, something like that. As long as they don't go after the family, what happens happens.

"Patriarch." Ma states. "The brothers are still out for blood. The father can be negotiated with. He has more experience with bloodshed and resolution than they do."

* * * *

Ma sent out the negotiation message a few hours ago. We've yet to receive a reply, but the older Dreadwals know their shit. They know that if they start a war it will ruin more lives than it will avenge.

I can hear Praxis and Alex discussing something in the other room, although it's hushed. The door is cracked open, letting bits of their conversation slip out on occasion. The only words that stick out to me are, "You can't go until this is resolved."

The girl might actually be considering leaving, if I'm not mistaken. Alex and I have talked about her enough before for me to know that she sure as hell didn't take on this life by choice. Maybe she can get out of it.

"They sent their reply." Ma enters the living room, taking a seat in her armchair under the rakia head. Me, the chief and Aunt Kaer all turn our attention to her. She calls for Alex and Praxis and me hear their conversation cut short.

They rush from the room and draw eyes on Ma. She taps her ringed fingers along the wooden end of the chair's extending arm, taking a deep breath. "They *will* be willing to negotiate peace," She looks almost sorry for the entire situation, as if retaliating were a bad idea. "If Allun goes to Sar Drea to face justice."

"Done." I say without even wincing. You know how shaky people get when they're scared? That's not what I'm feeling right now.

"You're just going to throw yourself to the Dreadwals?" Alex asks, concerned for his big brother.

It may be kind of selfish to toss my life away like it was nothing, but I've done enough for the family that I can do it with a clear conscience. If they kill me, so be it. If they put me in prison, their prisoners will most likely try to kill me. I've been in more than one prison before. Granted, the prisons I was in were more ship holding cells and military prison, but I get the basic premise.

"It's better than a war." I say as I light another cigarette, slowly killing my lungs. I swear, something's going to kill me one way or another before I've lived the full course of my life. I've done all the right things for it.

"You might actually survive a war, Allun!" He argues.

I shake my head. "At what cost? The expense of hundreds, maybe thousands of Vortigan soldiers? No. I'll face their justice system myself." I feel like my argument is the most reasonable here.

"Praxis, you're going with him." Ma demands.

Praxis looks to her curiously. "I'm not one to dispute orders," She says, "But I have to ask: *why*?"

Ma's breathing is heavy, which is apparent as the room goes quiet. She eyes Praxis, but her head doesn't move to face her. She closes her eyes after a moment, leaning her head back. "Because I need to make sure that there's a witness to what Allun did and someone to guard him until it's time for the trial. I can't very well send him marching in with soldiers. That would be suspicious. Sending a witness with him is the perfect cover for a bodyguard." She inhales deeply as I try to keep my cigarette back from her. "So, Allun... You're going?"

"I suppose so." I lean back against the wall and smile at Praxis. "Get ready for a flight."

* * * *

"She's... probably not going to make it through the night." The doctor tells me woefully, standing at the back of the room.

He hasn't made eye contact with me since I entered the room. Everyone in Sar Vort seems to know about my temper at this point.

Rin's face is almost unrecognizable, her hair partially burned, a good portion of her body no longer functioning. Those bastards got her good. They say she hasn't been able to speak, and she's been drifting in and out of consciousness.

"Her body is starting to shut down. The best I can say is that she'll be at peace."

"Going by a human standard, doctor," I correct him, "She won't be at peace. She'll be burning in Hell."

Human mythology was always so fascinating to me. Violence, rape, death; they're all very prominent on Earth. You'd expect their mythologies, then, their ideas of the afterlife to be somewhat peaceful. This is not the case in the slightest. Tartarus is plagued by those things-- no, Tartarus runs based on those things--and yet our mythology is very optimistic in comparison. If you buy into that rakia shit over at the Unified Church of Ocentarius, we all go, no matter our deeds, to the great Industrial City of Oceia. A city with willing slaves for every Tartuan, eternal happiness and no conflict. That's a load of Astarian shit, if you ask me.

"I... I'm sorry, sir, I didn't mean to-"

"You didn't offend me by being hopeful, doctor." I relieve him of any fears he may have had. "You're doing your job. I admire that. I just hated this bitch and I don't mind seeing her go. The woman I married died years ago."

I have no way of telling if she heard that, but it doesn't matter either way. It wouldn't change her opinion of me in the slightest. I turn back to the doorway and exit the compact little hospital room.

* * * *

I stand at the docks with Praxis, gazing over the edge. My family stands behind me--my mother, my little sister, my little brother; no sons to speak of. Smoke rolls out of my mouth as I flick the cigarette off of the edge, down the cliff and into a small ravine just under the port.

Ma looks at me with one of the only two emotions she can seem to produce, and I can't tell which one it is. It could be approval that I'm owning up to what I did, or it might be disappointment that I fucked things up enough to get sent away in the first place.

"Suppose this is the last you bastards'll be seeing of my ugly face for a while." I laugh in poor taste, but no one else seems amused.

"Ah, if you are sentenced to get out, it'll go by like that." Alex tries to make light of the situation. If a bad thing comes on, maybe it'll end tends to be his mentality.

I don't carry the same hopefulness. If things get bad, just be glad they aren't getting worse tends to be more of my philosophy. I can see my sister drying her tears. The girl's always been treated like a kid her whole life. The poor girl probably doesn't even know what I'm going away for. I imagine when she asked, all Ma told her was 'family business.' She deserves to know some things, but she would be mortified if she knew the state I put that boy in before he died.

"The whole system is rakia shit." I spit off the side of the dock and pull the flask from my pocket, swigging it and feeling myself get dizzier. Half of me wishes I could just fall off of the edge in a drunken fit, but I'm not going to fuck over the family like that. That would mess up the whole plan. "He bombed our plant, I killed him and his accompanying soldiers. What's wrong with that?" I probably shouldn't talk about it in front of Orvia, but I can't help it. It's the topic at hand.

"Goodbye, Alex." Praxis says quietly, still business-as-usual. Alex kisses her on the forehead.

"Don't get killed, kid." He tells her. He turns to me and gives me a big hug and a kiss on the cheek. She boards, waiting by the door for me. "And you try not to die, too. I don't want you leaving me the only sane man in the family."

"I'm not sane," I half-joke, "And my sentence will be what it is."

After hugs and goodbyes with everyone, they wave me off. I need to say something memorable. This may be the last time I see them, or at least the last time in a while.

I light myself another cigarette, leaning out of the transport ship's door. I take the pack and toss them out to Alex, smirking. "Hey Alex, keep the home fires burning for me, will you?"

"Not a lot in here, is there?" Praxis asks rhetorically from within the ship.

I pull myself back into the ship and the door seals behind me. I take a seat and look around. The only passengers are me, Praxis, an older couple, a beautiful young stewardess, the pilot and (hopefully) the co-pilot. Eh, it's a small ship anyway.

"Hope you packed some books." She holds both of our bags. I know I took my books, not that I'd probably be keeping them with me in prison. "It's a hell of a long ride from here."

"You ever been on a three-month voyage, Allun?" Praxis asks me.

"That sounds fucking awful." I reply. She looks to me, bright-eyed, and smiles with a shrug. "I think I'll be fine."

9

Praxis

My lips press against the co-pilot's as I pin his wrists to the large crate that's fastened in beside us. He shakes nervously as I slowly release my grip, sliding my hand over his inner thigh.

The handsome young co-pilot closes his eyes and runs his hand down my lower back, grabbing my ass, while holding himself up against the crate with the other hand. I lean in, my chest pressing against his as I kiss him again.

I told Allun I survived a three-month voyage. I didn't quite tell him that *this* is how I did it. Some people read on long trips, I find myself a fling. Through moaning and kisses, the man releases the words, "Typically we don't let passengers into the--oh my God--into the storage area..."

"I'm not your typical passenger." I say, planting another kiss on his lips. "You won't get in trouble for letting me back here."

"Y-you mentioned that."

I kiss him again. It's a long one this time. I tease him for a moment then begin unbuttoning his blue collared shirt, revealing a white undershirt. "Wh-who exactly are you?"

I try for the next three buttons, fumbling with them as I kiss him, bite his ear, his neck. He smiles at me, passion in his eyes, but still awaiting explanation.

"Vortigan Justicar," I tell him, getting the last three buttons undone. I help him pull the shirt over his head and begin unbuttoning my suit jacket as he throws his shirt off to the side. "Here on business."

"No way," He says and I kiss him again, grabbing him by the neck and holding him down onto the crate. I kiss him again while keeping him pinned. "That the story you tell all the guys you seduce?"

"It's true." I say and kiss him on the neck, up his cheek, on his mouth. I lean in and bite his ear. "What can I say? I'm dangerous."

* * * *

The co-pilot fixes his messy hair and begins buttoning up his shirt again, smiling at me. It was a pleasant way to spend a flight, but the flight is up. Fourteen hours of on-and-off 'occupying time' with the co-pilot. Finally, we've reached Sar Drea. I give the co-pilot a kiss, tell him that he should tell the pilot that it was a justicar and that I better not see him getting into any trouble for joining me in the storage area, then head up into the passenger section with him. I see Allun putting away his book as the ship lands, stuffing it into his bag, hoisting it up and handing me mine.

I wave goodbye to the co-pilot and step out of the ship with Allun and the old couple. Sar Drea, I notice, looks a lot like Sar Vort. It has bustling docks, slave traders waiting for their next shipment to arrive, the city in a bubble of smog. Several Dreadwal soldiers stand on duty at the docks, and I immediately recognize a man ahead of us as a Dreadwal Justicar. The old couple disperse to whatever location they had in mind, leaving Allun and me to be faced with the Dreadwal justice system.

"Allun Vortigan," The justicar speaks up. He looks like a weasel, tall and thin, protruding features around his mouth and nose, tall looking face. "You are suspected of murdering Teris Dreadwal. We demand that you come with us to face justice before Dreadwal Patriarch Torius Dreadwal the Second."

"I'm not *suspected* of murdering him," Allun corrects. "I openly admitted to doing the fucking deed. Check your facts."

Allun sighs and shakes his head, reaching for a cigarette and then remembering that he tossed them to Alex. I can tell that he regrets that decision now. "We're coming, asshole, alright?" The justicar stops him as he approaches and points to me.

"Your companion." He doesn't even say a full sentence when asking about me. I feel almost insulted. I flash my badge and step forward.

"I am Vortigan Justicar Praxis and I suggest that you address me directly." I threaten without making a direct threat. He glares at me and opens his mouth, but Allun waves down, ordering me to stop taking a defensive position. I do as told, taking a more quiet and passive tone. "And, also, witness to the death of Teris Dreadwal."

"Your justicar is your witness?" The Dreadwal justicar asks, turning his attention to Allun.

Allun nods, staring coldly at him. "Pardon my saying so, but that seems like a bad idea."

"She's the sole witness to the death of Teris." Allun growls and the justicar shrugs, urging us on.

* * * *

"Master Torius, we bring you-"

"Allun Vortigan, your son's killer." Allun interrupts the justicar, obviously fed up with all of this pomp and circumstance.

I honestly can't say that I blame him, with the trial being immediately after the flight. We stand in a large warehouse filled with a line of Dreadwal soldiers, several chairs lined up and several crates of chains and cuffs. Allun stares directly into the eyes of Torius, while I keep my eye on his sons. They both appear to be cuffed to their chairs, beside their father. They flail and argue, barking threats at Allun and me. Torius sighs.

"These boys are... far too violent." Torius grumbles, running his hand through his faded, dark gray hair.

The brother to the left of him falls over in his chair, yelling and trying to scoot toward Allun. A soldier lifts up the chair from the back, to avoid the horrible bite wounds that the boy would no doubt inflict on him.

"That was our little brother you killed, you son of a bitch!" The brother on the right spits at Allun, still shaking. They try hard to break free of their bindings, but to no avail.

"I brought you boys here to see how to handle passing judgment on a situation without emotional investment," Torius groans, "but it's obvious that my words fall on deaf ears. Take the boys out of the room. Their yelling is making me irritable."

"This guy killed Teri, Pa!" Screams the oldest of the two but, again, to no avail.

The soldiers hoist the chairs up with the boys on them and carry them from the room, despite the kicking and screaming.

"Maybe one day you two will learn what a justice system is!" Torius barks at them before turning back to us.

He bites his lip and shakes his head. "Damn kids. You got any kids?" He makes small-talk with Allun, who just looks away sadly in response. "War get 'em?"

He nods silently, trying to cover up his emotion, unsuccessfully. "I apologize for your loss. I've lost three to war myself. It appears I've lost another one to you."

"After I lost a lot of good men due to him." Allun defends his point, which Torius doesn't appear to be blind to. He nods, stroking his thick beard. "Justicar Praxis is a witness to my testimony."

"Your justicar is your witness?" He asks, almost impressed at the gall that Allun has to use me as his sole witness. "Does it not appear that she would have a bias?"

"I can't blame you for being suspicious," Allun shrugs, "but I don't have any non-biased witnesses. Any witnesses on your side would have jumped in front of the blaster shots I took at him when he tried to run. I think I-"

"No they wouldn't have." Torius interjects. "They would have let those shots hit my boy and end his life. Of course, blaster shots aren't what killed my son, are they?"

Allun shakes his head emotionless. He wasn't the one that fired the blaster shots, though. Of course it wouldn't help our case if he said I did it. "No, they wouldn't appear to be." Allun answers objectively.

I still remember the bruised, bloody, broken corpse of Teris Dreadwal. I can't say that it doesn't make me smile at least a little bit, though, that Teris met with some sort of early end. He was a racist little shit who considered Alkin and humans one and the same.

"The cause of death isn't very apparent, is it?" Torius grumbles.

Allun shakes his head. "No sir, it is not." He doesn't have much to say at this trial. I think the remark about his children ruined his will to speak up. He lost three sons, one by my hand. He understands what grieving Torius is going through well. His eyes light up for a moment. "But you will find that there isn't a single bullet hole on your boy's body."

"You're right." Torius nods. "I already noticed that. So it wasn't war you anticipated?"

"No sir." Allun stares the man in the eyes, not willing to look dishonest in the slightest. The old man's faded, but still very much alive, eyes meet Allun's in a mutual agreement of respect.

"Simply justice for the death of my men."

"And yet you killed more of my men than you'd needed to. They didn't give the order, did they?" Torius asks in the tone of a passive-aggressive parent.

I never like it when people take that tone, but I have to forgive it in this instance.

"What does your witness have to say on the subject?"

"Go ahead and tell him the truth, Praxis." Allun turns to me.

I can feel all of the eyes of Dreadwal soldiers on me, waiting for an answer on the death of their friends and brothers. Allun nods to me.

"Allun fought with your men because he believed that all of the Dreadwal soldiers--as few as there were--within the city were part of the plot. If they were conspiring against the Vortigan family, they were a threat. Your son corrupted his view of them." I answer, looking back. The eyes are still emotionless. I look back to Torius, who nods.

"Fair enough," He says and then shakes his head, "But the majority of the men you killed were innocent. I will not punish you for the death of my son, but you will have to serve some sentence for my men's lives."

"I'm willing." Allun nods to him.

"Fifteen years." Torius nods to Allun. "You may not bring personal belongings into the prison. You will serve your sentence here, in Sar Drea. You will be placed in a solitary cell so that your cellmates do not attempt your life, but you will eat and socialize around the other inmates. Fair?"

"Fair."

* * * *

"This isn't going to be too bad." Allun says to me as he removes his undershirt, revealing his surprisingly in-shape body.

He tosses the shirt and undershirt into a bin with his bag and all of its belongings. He hands in a holdout knife that was tucked into his pants, and they place it in its own box, sliding it into a drawer behind the desk. He begins unbuckling his belt, tosses it into the bin and yanks his pants down around his ankles. "You know, Praxis, this whole situation could have been avoided if I had control over myself."

He wiggles out of the leg holes and pulls down his boxers. I try not to look down.

"I didn't really control my own fate. I let instincts do all the work."

"Is that everything?" The Warden asks, looking into the bin.

Allun holds up a hand and shushes him. "Can't you see I'm talking, asshole? Yeah, that's everything."

The Warden approaches a closet on the other side of the room and pulls out a prison jumpsuit. He begins holding them to Allun's back, trying to get a measurement for which one might fit. The one he holds is obviously too long in the sleeves.

"Now, the same way my instincts control me, you're letting the family control you."

"I'm trying not to." I retort.

He nods, a knowing smirk growing on his face. "I know you're trying. I heard you and Alex talking." He says and I almost feel a sense of fear. No one was supposed to hear us talking, but he seems to have picked up on it. I hope to God the matriarch didn't. "If you plan on leaving, I have to ask that you do something that allows you to serve yourself before anyone else. Join a pirate crew, or become a bounty hunter, do something for *you*. I've seen too many soldiers just like you. Following orders, regulations, abiding by codes. I don't like it. You serve yourself first, then the ones you love. Next to serve are the ones you're okay with. Next, the friendly strangers. Last are the assholes and enemies. You understand my meaning here, Praxis?"

"You... You want me to control my own fate?" I ask, although the meaning is obvious.

He smiles. "You have so much potential, if you just use it. You don't belong stuck up in the cage of a Tartuan organized family like I'm in. You spread your wings, or whatever the hell it is people say in these speeches. You go out there and you take the fucking galaxy by storm. Look, I haven't known you that long, but something about me likes you. Go out there and find yourself some happiness. God knows I should have done it years ago."

Finally, the warden finds a fitting jumpsuit. Allun slides it on, rolls up his sleeves, loosens his collar and grins as the doors on the other side of the room swing open. He looks back at me and nods. "Don't get trapped, like me."

* * * *

The flight back to Sar Vort is long. Far too long, as I see it. No sex with the co-pilot, or the steward, or even any of the passengers. Just quiet reading and pondering between naps.

I realize that I'm not going to be a Vortigan justicar anymore, and I'm sure as hell not going to have the authority I have. I know everything about the trade and little about any other. I'm going to be so restricted to the trade itself that I won't be able to find a job anywhere else. I consider my options. Where can I go next? My home is no longer occupied by humans, and I'm assuming that its current Dreadwal owners have brought the law back.

Whatever happened to Zeph? Or Calypso? I know nothing about my best friends anymore. I don't how many of them lived; I don't know what happened to Zeph in that prison or what happened to Cal after that one news interview I saw, where he was helping people as best he could. Calypso, the last I checked, was terrified of what might happen to Aeson while he was in prison. I heard he was released, but I have no idea what he might be doing now.

I take my wrist communicator and immediately begin digging. I search through social networks, through communicator numbers, through everything I can to try and figure out what might have happened.

It's taken me years to pick up on this. Buried memories and fear for what I might learn have stopped me for so long, but I'm finally doing it.

I search for Aeson. I find a few articles on him, reading them on the small screen that sits on my wrist. I read comments on why he makes for a terrible General and arguments on what makes him a good General, but nothing useful.

I keep digging and digging until I reach a name on some social network. *Calypso Agaepto*. They got married.

I smile and shoot a message titled "anonymous," although I do state who I am in the message itself. I look at the picture of her and smile, tears filling my eyes. She's so much older and she's grown to be so beautiful.

Calypso.

It's been several years. I've been through some of the longest, most heartbreaking years of my life since I last saw you. We were best friends and I can only hope that you remember me.

It's Praxis. I still vividly remember how the war tore us apart. A lot of lives were lost in that war, but I can rest assured knowing yours wasn't. I'm curious, though. How is your brother? And Aeson? My God, I can just see how different our lives are now through your picture. You're older and smiling.

I, myself, don't smile that much anymore. I haven't really had the opportunity. So how did Alkineth react to discovering alien life? Or should I say IT discovering US? I discovered it shortly before all of you, so I guess I was just lucky.

I know that you have your own life and seeing someone you probably haven't thought about in years more than likely isn't your top priority, but I'd love to come back to Alkineth to see you, if you'll let me. I'd like to catch up.

Tears pour from my eyes and I cup my face in my hands as the message sends. I stare at the picture for a little while longer. Why didn't I consider this sooner?

Act I: Epilogue

Alex

"Christ alive," I smile, hugging Praxis tightly before she leaves aboard another space ship. A much bigger one, this time.

She handed in her badge to me earlier, and I told Taius that Praxis was no longer to be our justicar. Whether or not she is, I convinced Taius to still let her keep her penthouse suite free of charge. I want her to visit as often as she can.

"You have grown so much. I... You're not my kid, but I raised you, and I... I am so proud of you." I almost shed a tear. I've seen this girl almost every day of my life since I saved her, and now she's leaving.

"Thanks for everything, Alex." She kisses me on the cheek and steps aboard the ship, waving me off.

It's not bad enough that my brother goes to prison, but my would-be daughter has to ship off, too? I sigh and turn back to the docks. Slaves are prodded into their cages and wheeled off in trucks. I light one of Allun's cigarettes and examine Sar Vort. *I don't know if I really want to spend the rest of my life in the company of these people.*

END OF ACT I

ACT II

10

Praxis

"I thought I heard the old man say, 'leave her, Johnny, leave her! Tomorrow ye will get yer pay and it's time for us to leave her! Leave her, Johnny, leave her! Oh, leave her, Johnny, leave her! For the voyage is long and the winds don't blow and it's time for us to leave her!'"

The spacers sing, loudly and drunkenly, although I can't say that they don't have passion in their songs. The ship soars slowly, releasing a low hum as we drift into view of Alkineth. I almost find myself crying at the sight of that little, insignificant blue marble in a whole galaxy of far larger worlds. I would cry if it weren't for the fact that I'm surrounded by spacers. Judgmental, tough-as-nails (or at least they like to think so) spacers.

Several ships hover around Alkineth, moving slowly, some finding themselves moving toward the world, some away from it and others simply sitting in place. Three stations appear to have been built around it now, small but bustling.

I wipe sweat from my forehead and grin, happy to see my home. It's been far too long since I've seen my own people. Sure, I've seen the occasional Alkin or Space-Born out in the void of space or some arriving on Proscriptus, but they certainly aren't common. Despite contact with the Tartuans, we definitely haven't gotten our feet off of our home ground quite yet.

Last I checked, Alkin was in a strong alliance with the Dreadwals, seeing as they were the first ones to land and we didn't ask questions. I remember the political promises the Dreadwals made from news stories. A speech was given by Torius Vortigan himself on the subject of the invasion. He convinced our people that backing the Industrial Empire was the wisest decision we could make, especially if we planned on retaliating against the humans. Just like a Tartuan Leading Family to exploit a war during the aftermath recovery stage. I will admit that from what I've seen, they have helped us recover quite a bit. The cities were very efficiently rebuilt thanks to the help of androids that they kept working day and night, as well as Astarian slaves working in factories to keep production stable, as well as slaves being sold to farmers to keep the food growing, medicine and immigrated doctors to keep the population healthy, not to mention limitless new knowledge.

All of this comes cheap from Tartarus, though. To the Dreadwals, and even the Industrial Empire as a whole, this wasn't helping a devastated population reconstruct society; all they were doing was taking another world for themselves without having to put in the extra effort of invasion. Despite having spent a lot of time among Tartuans and gaining an appreciation for their culture, I've found that their politics make me frown and scowl.

My eyes never leave the little blue ball, scanning it over and over again. I smile and force my eyes shut for just a moment to think back on the time I've spent on this world. I think back to my would-be boyfriend, Zeph, the most. His plot for revenge, that passionate fire in his eyes; everything about him seemed so appealing when I was young. Now that I look at it with an experienced eye, I don't care for his ideas. He got himself arrested in a makeshift attempt to kill a man who, in the long run, wouldn't have had any effect on the course of the war. It makes me sick to even think it, but the fact is that Zeph was a foolish teenage boy who got himself caught up in something he didn't understand. I thought I loved him back then, but I've pondered it the entire voyage. I wasn't in love with him, I just thought he was hot and had a slight affection.

When I think back, I was a different person. If I'd known him now, I'd say he got what he deserved by getting arrested. You don't create an assassination plot the night before you attempt it. It requires planning and professionalism; Zeph lacked both of these. He was an ignorant, angry boy who happened to get caught up in a situation that allowed him to express his rage.

This revelation came to me shortly before we reached sight of Alkineth, as if the world itself brought it on. Hell, maybe it did.

I turn my attention from the world to the bar behind me. The ship's bar is spacious and filled to the brim with off-duty engineers, guards and travelers like myself. I volunteered for a job as a guard if they'd take me to Alkineth on their next voyage, which my previous status as a Vortigan Justicar granted me. The voyage took a few weeks, but we're finally here. We'll probably dock within the day.

I sit down at the bar and stare at the TV, which is set on the Intergalactic Sports Station. There happens to be a match going on right now between a human boxer and one of an Outer-World race called the Sprites that I've been seeing more and more of lately.

Hell, two of the servers in the ship's bar are Sprites. What brings an Outer-World race to spread like they have, I'm not sure. They're an interesting folk, but not the strangest I've seen.

Their biology is something like I've never seen, being somewhere between plant and animal in terms of physical attributes. Rather than hair, they have petals like a flower, florescent green skin (at least the ones I've seen) and I've heard they've got some pretty bulbous parts below the metaphorical belt. Technically they're still classified as an animal life form. I'm no scientist, though, so I couldn't tell you how they function.

All of this thinking about them makes my eyes and mind both drift toward them. I glance at the young Sprite waiter, who rushes from table to table, serving the off-duty spacers. One rather blunt human woman smacks him on the ass as he makes his run for more drinks.

The yellow-petaled Sprite boy makes an expression of disgust and I feel sympathy. Allun's son, Walder, treated me the same way before I cut off his fucking head. No one should be treated like that. "Hey, waiter," I say and wave him over.

He approaches me with his notepad open and his pen ready. "What do you need?" He asks me pleasantly. His English is fine, but his accent needs some work. He's a bit hard to understand at first hearing.

I shake my head and put a hand on his notepad, lowering it. "Look, kid, I saw her smack you on the ass like that and I saw the face you made. You want me to handle it?"

"I..." He goes quiet and looks over at her, then turns back to me. "Handling one situation won't solve anything. I can take the harassment."

He tries to turn away, but I put my hand on his arm and urge him to turn back to me. "You *don't* have to take the harassment. Stick up for yourself." I advise him, worried for his safety. If he doesn't start sticking up for himself, God knows what people might do to take advantage of him. "I used to have a guy that would always harass me and even tried to rape me at one point."

"What did you do?" The Sprite boy asks me, simultaneously intrigued by the story and horrified by the event that occurred.

I look him in the eyes and show no expression. "Well, first his adopted older brother tried to stop him. Of course, he didn't respect his adopted brother. Hell, no one did, not even their father. Oelicus was pretty much just a backup-heir, not even considered a son by his adopted father, Allun. Well, this guy--who tried to rape me--eventually had a price put on his head. I went and collected it. I shot him, repeatedly, until he was finally in enough pain that I was satisfied. So, I cut off his head."

The Sprite now looks terrified at my recount of the story.

"But for you, I'd recommend taking some martial arts classes."

* * * *

I stand at the Alkineth docks and look around at my would-be home. It's so much different than I remember it. Of course, what I remember was mostly rubble.

The war has blocked most of my memory of my home-world that didn't take place during it. All I remember of the world before is my mother giving me strawberries when I was about four or five years old. *Damn, I could go for some strawberries.*

I begin paying attention to the people around me; who they are, what they're doing, it's all fascinating to me. A podium with an auctioneer behind it stands further up, almost off of the docks. He's selling spaceship parts, Astarian slaves, furniture, probably whatever he could get off the back of a cargo ship. On another side of the dock, soldiers are returning home. Alkin soldiers leave their ship, smiling and hugging those waiting for them on the other side. A young man and a young woman immediately begin kissing, passionately and almost aggressively.

I turn back away. Two spider-bodied androids with more humanoid features protruding upward help an old Undrian man with his bags. Dreadwal officers work alongside Alkin security workers, searching bags and checking humans' papers. I think that it's because I'm Alkin that they don't care to search me. It's a horrible bias, but I'm not going to complain. They're mostly searching the humans and, while I'm sure those humans are innocent, I can understand why they would do that. I may not agree with it, but I understand it. The war hasn't exactly shed humans in a good light.

I glance up at the big, beautiful blue sky and watch as more ships ascend and descend, going to and fro, all ending up in God-knows-where. Another role played by the color blue: our world's skies and oceans.

I look back down and gaze across the dock. I see, approaching from the front, Calypso. She grins, tears in her eyes, and runs across the docks toward me. I can't help but smile and cry in return. She was always like a sister to me. Seeing her now is... It's simultaneously joyous and heartbreaking.

I clutch her like I've never clutched anyone, not wanting to let go. I don't want to let go of her again.

"Jesus Christ, it's been so long..." She cries on my shoulder, shaking her head and laughing.

I was almost worried that it'd been so long that she'd forgotten about me, but it doesn't seem to be that way. I'm glad it isn't. "I thought you might have died. I thought of you when Cal had a candlelight vigil for the ones that went missing and were never found..." I wipe the tears from my eyes and pat her on the back. The hug lasts far, far longer than most hugs do.

She releases me and holds me by the head, staring into my eyes. "God, you've... You've gotten so much older." She laughs.

I laugh in return. "Look at yourself." I retort.

She finally releases me and leads me back to her car, urging me along.

I come with her gleefully, getting into the passenger side and taking a deep breath. It's good to see her again. "So where have you been?" She asks me.

I take a deep breath. "Well, I got smuggled off-world during the war and joined a Tartuan family for a while," I inform her, to her amazement. "But, well, I've retired from that. I'm trying to forge my own path, you could say."

"What family?" She asks me curiously.

"Vortigans. They were good to me. I probably wouldn't be alive right now if it weren't for them."

* * * *

Calypso stops for a few groceries before we head back to her house. Apparently, she and Aeson live in the Red Palace now. Aeson is the top-ranking general, and the very prospect of monarchy on the world seems to have been abolished. I honestly don't like it, though. The world's been privatized by the Dreadwals. My home is just another place to lay down factories for them.

The evening sky is gorgeous, with multicolored lights shimmering all over. It's been a long time since I've actually been able to *see* a sky. It's mostly been space and smog since I've left. The closest I get to seeing sky is on TV and space-port worlds that seem to be in a state of constant nighttime.

I step out of the car and look to the pharmacy ahead of us, reading the glowing signs that hang from the windows. *Open all day*, *prescriptions* and *we can refuse service to anyone.*

I follow Calypso into the little corner-store and smile at the man at the counter, nodding to him. He nods back, tips his hat and goes about his business. Calypso leads me to the back for a gallon of milk and some snack-cookies, putting them into her basket and turning to me. "Hey, Praxis, can you go get me some window cleaner? Aisle six."

I silently make my way over to find it. She didn't specify the brand, so I find myself staring at a row of window-cleaners and not knowing what to pick. Aisle six, given the size of this store, finds itself just against the wall opposite the entrance.

I hear the ding of the store's door opening. I glance over and see a young silver-eyed blue-blood, probably around twenty or so. He wears a beanie that covers his hair entirely and an over-sized coat with someone quite obviously protruding from the pocket. Through analysis I realize that he's most likely armed with a blaster, and this is most likely a robbery.

I keep my eye on him, but pretend to be paying attention to the cleaner. I look up at the security camera. He's standing right under it. They'll catch his face if he robs the store, but I don't think that's going to stop him. He's more than likely on Star. He has that look in his eyes. I've seen enough junkies come into Proscriptus to recognize it.

I feel myself inclined to grab the knife at my hip, but I'm not quite ready for it. I'll have to examine everything first.

He goes for the blaster. He yanks it from his pocket and aims it for the security camera. He blows a smoking hole in it, as if that's going to do anything to prevent them from finding him.

Calypso screams and ducks, dropping her milk and cookies. the pharmacist at the counter holds up his hands and I hold up mine just to pretend I'm going along with it. His hand is shaking, his aim is bad and the look on his face says he's never fired that thing once.

"Everybody be cool!" He yells out, looking around the store.

There are two other customers who have their hands up as well. He begins throwing out orders to everyone. Calypso and the other two get on the ground while the pharmacist begins emptying the register. I don't know if he's noticed me standing behind the rack in aisle six. It leaves me with a good opportunity.

I slowly creep to the edge of the aisle, waiting for him to take note. He doesn't seem to, though. "We can all make it through this alive if you-"

"If you put down the gun." I growl before coming around the corner.

He aims it at me, shaking and cowardly.

I step forward and he holds it out as if he's going to shoot. He might shoot if I scare him, but I've seen enough people like him to know that he'll give it away before he shoots. Calypso mouths my name, looking up at me from the back of her aisle. Her milk is leaking all over the floor, some soaking through her shirt.

"Back off, bitch," The robber continues to point it at me, or at least try to, but it's slightly to the left. His shot wouldn't even hit me. I put my hands up and step in a little closer to him until I'm right at the end of his barrel. "I will put a fucking hole in your head!"

"No you won't." I say, shaking my head. "You won't kill me. You've never killed anyone, and you're not going to make me your first. You can put down the gun and go home, or you can try and rob this store, although the camera's already seen your face."

"I already shot the camera!" He barks, trying to sound like he had a rational plan to begin with.

The more I look at him, the more I hear his lack of planning, the more he reminds me of Zeph. The difference, though, is that Zeph would pull that trigger.

"You and I both know that shooting that camera does not get rid of the footage that was already taken." I reason, "Just as well, you and I know that if you don't leave this store right now, a fate worse than arrest will befall you."

"What the fuck did you just-" I notice that his finger isn't even on the trigger anymore. It was getting sweaty, so he pulled it back off for a moment to rest it. Now's my chance.

I grab the blaster, twist it from his hand, click my finger on the safety and drop it to the ground. I use my other hand and go for the knife hidden at my waistline. I slide it out and bury the blade handle-deep into his throat, watching blood bubble up from his neck and mouth as he tries to claw at my arm. He leaves a few scratches, but no real marks.

Calypso, the pharmacist, and the other customers all scream.

He came in holding a gun and threatening people. Why are they all so upset now that he's dead?

* * * *

"Why did you do that?" Calypso asks me as we sit on the curb, waiting for the police.

The pharmacist, although horrified at how I handled the situation, seemed pleased that I'd saved his store and his money. He told me that, no doubt, his word would be worth more than any of the customers', so he'd vouch that I had no choice. Calypso will also vouch, despite being so horrified at what I did.

"He threatened us and tried to rob that poor pharmacist." I defend my point, although I'm second-guessing it just as well as her.

She shakes her head, wiping tears from her eyes. I suppose she thought she'd seen the last of bloody conflict.

"He held a blaster right to my face." I added.

"You said that he wouldn't have fired. Is that true?" She asks me and I begin to wonder. It was true, without a doubt, that he was all talk.

Why did I do it, then? Why did I kill him? Was it some inner hatred for Zeph that drove me, or was it simply instinct at this point? As the sirens blare and lights come in closer, I can hear the question still being begged. *Why did you do that?*

11

Allun

"My boys were soldiers," I say to my cellmate as I do push-ups to keep myself in shape.

Being in prison isn't going to make me lazy and I'm sure as hell not going to get out of shape and let it kill me. Also, for some reason I do have a cellmate. I could have sworn the old bastard said no cellmates. I'd file a complaint if this prison were of any quality.

The cell is small, concrete, dingy--sort of like Sar Vort, really. Most cities on Tartarus are just as bad as their prisons, so the prisons don't seem too bad in comparison. My cellmate is a convicted murderer, killed his neighbor after he caught him smacking his son around. Can't say I blame him, honestly. If I found out my boys were being beaten on, I'd have killed the person doing it as well. That being said, nobody would fuck with my boys because they were Vortigans. "Just like their old man."

"How many sons did you have?" He asks me, a cigarette hanging from his mouth as he leans against the wall. He has no way of lighting it, but I understand holding it in your mouth even if you can't smoke it. It's at least a little bit comforting.

"Well, legally, four. Biologically speaking, three." I grunt out the answer between breaths before finishing up my round of push-ups. I pick myself up and take a seat on my bunk, just across from his. He slides a cigarette out of the pack and tosses it over to me. I clench it between my

teeth and sigh. "Lost my youngest several years ago. Still haven't quite gotten over it."

"You never talk about your fourth." My cellmate speaks up, laying back against the wall on his side. He puts his hands on his stomach, locks his knuckles together and sighs. I shake my head and reach under my bunk, pulling out a book I had stashed away under there. A novel about pirates that I traded with a guy for a few smokes. The novel is shit, but it keeps me occupied.

"What's to talk about?" I shrug. "Oelicus is my backup plan, not my kid. Somebody's got to keep the name alive, but honestly? That boy isn't my kid. I didn't raise him. I adopted him just before he was a legal adult so I'd have someone to carry on the name. At that point, my oldest two were dead. I felt like I was cursed, you know? Had to have someone with barely any ties. Maybe then he'd carry on the name, even if he wasn't really mine."

"So your fourth is just business?" He asks me. I nod, opening up the book. "That's fucked up."

"Well nobody asked you."

* * * *

The food in here is absolute garbage. I wouldn't dare say it out loud because I'll take what I can get, but the food is shit. Lunch is probably the worst time of the day; not only because of the food, but because I've had people try to hit me during lunch three times since I've been here. I think the Dreadwal brothers called out an order to kill me and pulled some strings in the prison, but so far the only people that have tried it are drugged-up inmates. This means that every guard here is on their father's payroll. I'm glad, otherwise I'd have a few more holes in me than I'd like.

"Hey, uh, Allun Vortigan?" An inmate behind me in the lunch line asks.

I look over at him. A buff, empty-headed sack of shit. I've seen him around. He holds his hand behind his back, telling me he's got a weapon. I don't even answer him. A swift punch in the throat ends it faster than words will.

He falls to the ground choking, gasping and wheezing. Security rushes forward, one of them trying to save the man on the ground and two of them holding me back. I don't struggle. "Check his hand." I order and, although the guard doesn't want to listen to me, he does as instructed.

A blade, sure enough, crafted out of a sharpened brush.

"Are you going to pretend I did something wrong, or are we going to continue with lunch?"

The guards release me and drag away the man's fresh corpse, confiscating his blade. Inmates stare at me for the rest of lunch, but they've seen me kill at least three guys since I've been here. I don't know why they're still acting so surprised.

"Allun, man, that was cold." One of the guys who I play cards with says, taking a bite out of his sandwich.

I continue to eat in silence as the men around me chatter. I can here them all talking about me as if I wasn't here, but they don't say anything bad. It's mostly compliments to the balls it took to just kill the man without even thinking about it, people saying they would cross over to the other side if they saw me walking their way down the street, etc.

"How many people have you killed, Allun?" Another guy I play cards with asks curiously.

I look up to him and shrug. They all start to laugh, as if it's inconceivable that a man like me--one not in solitary, mind you--has killed that many.

"Seriously, like, you got a number?"

"I never counted, and I can't remember every single one." I sip water from the bottle I bought from the vending machine. "It's not something to brag about."

"I hear people brag about it all the time!" Someone at our table exclaims.

I shake my head and stare him in the eyes, unblinking. "Those guys that brag? They aren't professionals. They're either amateurs or they're nothing at all."

* * * *

Now on to the phones. I consider who I'm going to call, first. You only get so many call tokens in a week. I already called Alex and Ma this week.

I think maybe I'll call my buddy Pairus in the Rogue Agency. We grew up together, Pairus, Alex, Taius and I. We were the danger of the fucking neighborhood. We went where we pleased, we did what we pleased, we broke a few hands in our day. Alex, Taius and I all grew up to fit our predetermined roles. We would be family heads, as will every Vortigan family member with enough of a ruling personality. Pairus, though? None of us knew where he would go. I always figured that if the galaxy wasn't on his side, I would just give him a job.

Turns out, though, he's doing bigger things than even us. Pairus is a factor the Vortigans have that nobody else does. Pairus is a Rogue Agency fleet Admiral. He has strong ships, strong crews, his fleet embodies strength in and of itself.

The best thing about all of this is that he's on our side. Hell, I've been on his ship once or twice, I've seen his fleet. five-hundred ships strong (counting the smaller vessels) and armed to the teeth. All it would take is asking a favor and he could wipe out an entire fucking colony world. Granted, there would be repercussions with the Rogue Agency and Pairus would probably disappear, but the fact is that he would take that risk for us.

Pairus is a true friend. I consider what I might say to him. I'm not going to waste his time with just a casual call. He's Rogue Agency. He's got worlds to liberate and governments to control.

I think back on what might warrant a call. Any small favors I could ask, maybe. *Praxis*, I think in a moment of generosity. I could ask him to seek her out, maybe enlist her. Hell, she was Taius' justicar. With those credentials, she'll make captain in no time. The family owes her, anyway. After her years of loyal service, it's only fair that I get her a good job.

I pick up the phone and punch in his number. It rings for a minute and then I get him on the other end. His voice is rougher than I remember, but he's always had a rough voice. Maybe it's the same, and I just haven't heard him in a while.

"Who is this?" His gruff, smoky voice demands.

I hesitate to reply, but only because I'm lost in thought. "That how you talk to an old friend?"

The conversation that follows is one I'm happy to have. It goes on for at least an hour, talking about Praxis, about how I got locked up in a Dreadwal prison, how he almost got killed in a fight with some pirates the other day, how he's gone off and gotten married. It almost makes me feel out of touch with the world.

Eventually, the guards yank me away from the phones and I'm forced to cut it short. They send me back to my cell and I take some pride in the fact that my old friend is a Rogue Agency admiral. Maybe another friend of mine can be worked into the Agency somewhere. Hell, I bet Pairus could get me out of this prison if I asked him. But I'll make the wise move and do my time.

12

* *Praxis* *

"Picture me upon your knee with tea for two and two for tea! Just me for you and you for me!"

Calypso sings in a sweet tone far more mature than I remember from childhood as she pours tea for herself, Aeson, their children, Cal and I around the table.

I've been here for a few days now and I'm still not quite settled in. Cal has taken a leave from his soup kitchen--which he founded--for the night to have dinner with us. Despite the incident on my first day back, no one has treated me any differently. I guess the war desensitized most of them to, well, death. The fact that I killed that man was obviously viewed in a negative light, but I wasn't shunned. The war has obviously had a lasting effect.

Calypso wears a pretty white dress that goes just above her knees, with a long ponytail reaching down the back of her head. Their son, Neo and their daughter, Delilah, chatter to each other at the end of the table, sitting beside one another. Aeson has a seat open for Calypso to sit down next to him, while I sit beside Cal.

Cal looks unwashed, for the most part, but pleasant. His hair is unkempt and his clothes are practically rags, but that's probably intentional. The last I heard, he was standing up for the poor by giving away his belongings and founding a soup kitchen and a charity. Aeson is probably the richest person on Alkineth and has been fully supportive of Cal's endeavors. Galactic News tells you a lot when someone is in the public eye.

Aeson is strong-featured now, with his copper hair cropped. He's an acting general so I'd assume that's mandatory. He wears his uniform to dinner, but it's most likely because he just got home from giving orders in the barracks. Being stationed at home is probably pretty easy on him, not to mention he apparently inherited the damned world from that dead emperor.

Now Emperor Elagabalus is in power and he's... Not our worst, but certainly not our best. He's getting dicked by the Dreadwals left and right. He has no backbone.

"So, Praxis," Cal starts, looking over at me with a smile. I see a rosary hanging around his neck and realize something: Cal appears to have found religion. "Where have you been all these years?"

No sense in lying to everyone. "Well, I've been surviving." I tell them, with not much more to add to that. I don't want to lie, but I don't want to reveal the full truth. Why would I want to tell them that I killed people for a living?

I take a deep breath and think on what I'm going to say, because the looks on their faces--even the children--demand more. "I was a law-maker for a... for a Tartuan family."

"Law-maker? You mean a... What do they call it? Justicar?" Cal asks, hoping he's right.

I nod and confirm it, and he takes some pride in his cultural knowledge.

Aeson leans forward in his seat and looks to me as Calypso takes her seat by him. She pours her own tea last and begins sipping, watching us. I can hear chefs in the kitchen preparing food. Like I said, Aeson inherited the world. He's got his own chefs and servants to tend to his every whim. You'd never see that on Alkineth except in service of the emperor.

"Well, I'm actually pretty curious, I... I don't know much about the Tartuans. What's with these guys?" Aeson asks me, looking around.

I'm hesitant to say anything, but I do have my fears for what might happen to Alkineth if Tartuans get their hands on it legally. They won't enslave our people if we don't resist, but they certainly won't care for the poor and sick, the way Cal does, and will likely replace Aeson as a general.

I look around the table. I look to the kids. Innocent little red-eyed, black-haired children. They don't look like they're ready to know the truth. Neither do Cal and Calypso.

Aeson should know, though. I sigh and shake my head. "That will take a more private conversation to explain." I say honestly.

Calypso looks confused. Cal shrugs and begins drinking his hot tea. I look down at mine. Two sugar cubes float serenely in the tiny cup and I take a sigh. I begin to drink, my eyes darting around the bright room. The chefs break through the doors with a tray, laying out our food for us individually. Aeson and Calypso first, then the children, then me, then Cal last. They all rush back into the kitchen with their tray as quickly as they'd entered. We can't even hear them beyond the door anymore.

"So... What happened while I was gone?"

"Well, the Tartuans, for one." Aeson says bluntly, but I can see Calypso smack his side under the table. It did come off as rude, but I ignore it. I lived on Proscriptus. I'm used to rude. "In terms of the war? Um... I don't know how to tell you this..."

A death. It's going to be a death. Probably Zeph or Neo, most likely. Provided the context, it would have to be them. The only other death within the group was one I witnessed. The rest of us seem mostly unscathed here, other than a few scars. Scars have stories, though.

Judging by Aeson's, the prison of a human war-vessel wasn't too kind to him. These aren't scars you get through battle. Facial scars, neck scars, what appear to be claw scars down his hands. He's had it rough. "We found Zeph's body lying in a ditch just outside of the city."

"I can't say I'm surprised." I say, hardening myself to the news.

Part of me says I should react, but another part of me insists that I ignore the compassionate part. Zeph knew what he was getting into. If I show empathy, it's a weakness.

The boy faced a general and he lost. There's nothing else to him. He was the first boy I had, and I used to think he was the first boy I loved. But I didn't love him, I've decided. I couldn't have loved him. I thought I loved him because he was the most attractive person around me and I was a stupid girl. "He was campaigning to kill General Wolfe. Not something your average sixteen-year-old boy would be able to accomplish. I remember hearing his 'plan.' It was rushed and tactless."

They stare at me in absolute awe; they're stunned the cold nature of my statement. The kids don't seem to be paying much attention, as they chatter amongst themselves, but the adults are speechless.

I shrug, sipping my tea further. Eventually, Calypso speaks up. "Well, you two *did* kind of have a thing, I... I just figured you'd be a little more shocked, if you didn't already know."

"The years have given me time to consider the possibilities and probabilities. There was a possibility that he survived his imprisonment after attempting to assassinate General Wolfe, but the probability was that he was killed in prison. The fact that we had a 'thing' does not mean anything. We were kids. I won't forget our time together, but I won't pretend he didn't have a death wish. Still, if he... If he has a grave, I'd like to visit it."

I wouldn't, actually. But I tell them this so that I don't seem so alien to their feelings. I don't think Proscriptus had the best influence on me, now that I see myself attempting to connect to people who didn't grow up in Tartuan society.

Even the kids seem to be paying attention now. Neo is ten and Delilah is eleven, so they're close enough in age that I can treat one the same way I treat the other. Maybe hearing this won't be too damaging.

"He's, uh... He's buried out in a nearby cemetery. We'll take you there after dinner." Aeson says, looking over to Calypso.

She looks a bit shocked, but not quite offended. Aeson understands. I can hear it in his voice and read it on his face. He's a soldier, though. Another hardened soul, whether his family knows it or not. His youth and innocence were probably tortured out of him.

* * * *

We stand at the site of the grave, and I can only look over the epitaph and stare blankly. '*He died for his home.*'

Bullshit. Pretentious and untrue bullshit. Zeph died for his pride and his quest for meaning. He died for the idea that me might be revered as a hero. History will forget him and rightfully so. He doesn't deserve to be remembered and revered. Hell, he doesn't deserve an epitaph. The most he deserves is his name marked on the gravestone and the date of birth and death. I don't even remember when he was born. I sure as hell don't know when it was he died.

"Well, this is it, then."

"This is it." Cal says, putting his hand on my shoulder.

Calypso hugs me, expecting me to break down, but I just stand and stare. Mourning would be useless. I don't remember anything about him as a person. All I remember is his pride and his attempt at glory. Objectively speaking, he isn't deserving of glory. He did nothing but march in without a plan and try to blow a hole in the general. That doesn't deserve memorial.

"You alright?"

"I'm fine." I say, turning around.

I look up at the twinkling white-and-blue stars above us. I see a red one off in the distance and wonder what it could be. I've never seen a star like it and I never was one for the scientific side of the galaxy. The way things work has never interested me as much as what their function is meant to be. If knowledge of a red star won't benefit me, why care?

"We should all get back. It's late." I've spent enough time around Zeph in my lifetime. I don't need to be around him any longer.

* * * *

I sit in the the living room and stare into the fireplace, sighing. A deer head is mounted on the wall over my chair, and a portrait hangs over the fireplace of Emperor Sebastian. The glow of the fire shines onto it and makes it gleam.

Sebastian's chiseled features are on display, being right above the only light source in the room. I can see a light come on just down the hall. I consider my old friend and hope somewhat that it's her. We haven't gotten to connect much since I've returned to Alkineth, and I'd really like that. As the footsteps get heavier, I realize that it's not Calypso. I don't know why I would have expected it to be in the first place, honestly. She sleeps so heavily she wouldn't be up and walks so lightly that I wouldn't know she was even up anyhow.

Instead, the much taller, stronger body of Aeson enters the room. He's wearing a t-shirt and gray pajama pants. Not what I expected, given how rich he seems to be.

He takes a seat in an armchair across the room from mine, staring at Sebastian on the wall. The glow of the fire starts to dim and Sebastian's head is no longer in our line of view.

"You know," Aeson says quietly, not wanting to wake anyone. His voice in whispers is almost as soft as it was when he was young. "Sebastian was the closest thing I had to a dad. Sure, I had my biological father, but he didn't respect me in the slightest. Sebastian treated me like I was a goddamn prince. He left me this house, for Christ's sake. I bet he would have named me his legal son if he'd lived for it."

"Yeah, I've... I've got someone like that." I say, thinking back to Alex.

Alex never treated me like royalty, but he did treat me as his equal. I'm hoping to see him again sometime soon. I need to keep in touch with him, but it's difficult. He's all the way in Tartarus or Proscriptus or... somewhere. "Alex is the reason I survived the war, an adopted son of a Tartuan matriarch. He's Alkin, himself. He smuggled me off-world and got me a job. It paid well. It kept me in one place most of the time. I could make some of the rules, but I always had to answer to a boss. If I had any problems, any solution was feasible. It was nice."

"So what made you leave?" He asks, leaning back in his seat.

I sigh and shrug, not knowing what to tell him. Sometimes I don't know what to tell myself.

"Sounds like you had it made. No disrespect, of course. I'm sure you had your reasons."

"It wasn't me." I tell him, finally coming up with an answer that suits me. It's the truth, or at least part of it. The situation is far too complex for words to describe. "The fact is, I wasn't an individual. I followed orders. My orders were to call the shots, so I did; only, the shots weren't mine to call. I acted as a hand for my bosses. Anything I did, it had to go by them first."

"Sounds like my job." He smirks, leaning back. He closes his eyes and takes a deep breath. I notice for the first time that his breathing sounds off. Probably a wound he's suffered, although he's breathing at a normal pace. The sound of the breaths themselves seems almost mechanical. "So, where are you going to go now?"

"Well, I can't stay here forever." I say with an exhausted sigh and a yawn. I'm getting tired, but I'm not ready to go to bed. I need to sort things out.

"To put it bluntly, no. You can't." He says blatantly. "I'm sorry, that came off ruder than I'd intended. What I'm saying is that this house already has one professional killer in it. The difference, though, is that my training actually taught me how to hold a guise of humanity when I returned to society. Yours sticks with you."

"What would you advise?" I ask for his expert opinion.

He opens his eyes back up and yawns, stretching his arms out. He looks to me and puts his hand on his chin.

"Well, a woman like you could always find herself a job as a bounty hunter, or maybe a privateer." He says with a smile. He laughs to himself a bit before opening his mouth again. "I'd recommend soldier but... Well, that's my job talking."

"Bounty hunter, huh?"

"Sure. I'll write you up a letter of recommendation first thing tomorrow, and you can head over to the office and get your license. Trust me, if I recommend you, no way they'll refuse. You know what?" He thinks on it for a moment. "Fuck the letter. I will personally drive you to the office and get you that license. Now I'm gonna get some sleep."

* * * *

Aeson did as he'd promised and got me a license without any hassle.

He headed on to the barracks afterward and left me at the buildings, with my permission to leave, of course. I am now the proud owner of a Hunter's License. I can capture wanted criminals and carry military-grade weaponry and it's perfectly legal, now.

I walk down a long, narrow corridor that almost resembles a hospital, with gray walls and a shiny white floor that's constantly being cleaned by various janitorial androids. A spider-android of obvious Tartuan design spits soap onto the floor as his legs tap against the porcelain. A tall clockwork android moves his awkward legs behind him, mopping the floor up. It's always been amazing to me to see advancements like this in Tartaun society. Their technologies are constantly being improved upon, and their empire constantly growing because of it.

Tartuan imperialism is a bittersweet thing. On one end, it provides the worlds it attaches itself to with all new technologies and means of defense as well as knowledge. On the other hand, those who refuse to accept it are massacred and enslaved. These androids symbolize either a tremendous golden age for Alkineth's culture, or the end of it.

At the end of the bright, shimmering hall I reach an elevator. I hit the button and wait for at least a minute before it actually reaches me. The doors slide open and I step on immediately, pressing the button. "*Eighteen,*" I mutter to myself, trying to remember my floor number, eighteen or nineteen. I hit eighteen hesitantly. The doors shut, and the elevator starts going up, but it stops after just one floor.

The doors slide open and I look out. There stands a short man coated in makeup. He has shining golden lip gloss, dark eye-liner and perfect, wavy long hair. His bright green eyes dart about the elevator before stepping on.

I notice his clothing; that is to say, I notice his flamboyance. He wears a bright red waistcoat over a golden waistcoat, a cravat and old-style breeches. The most modern thing about him appears to be his black boots, but even they still look somewhat colonial.

He looks to me and smiles before running his hand over the number pad and punching his button. *Nineteen.*

"Hello there!" He says, stepping back.

"Hi." I wave back to him, my gaze staying trained on him.

The eighteenth floor seems so far away right now as I stand in lingering silence. Eventually, I open up conversation. "So, um... Forgive me for asking but... What exactly is it you do here?"

"I'm renewing my contract." He says, as if I should get it.

I'm still absolutely befuddled as to why the living hell he's dressed like that. Eventually he realizes that I didn't catch on. "I'm, uh... I'm a privateer captain." He explains to me.

I nod, leaning back against the elevator door. *Where is that fucking floor?* "I'm guessing you're a bounty hunter?"

"How can you tell?"

"Well, you didn't recognize what I meant by 'contract.' People of your profession don't pick up contracts, just warrants. Do you know your mark? I've traveled and I've met some people; I might be able to help you out." He offers, although I don't know my mark at all.

I know my location. "Don't know my mark, but I know where I'm headed. Floor eighteen takes me to the Seregua offices, which means they've figured out that that's where he's holed up. It's just a matter of dispatching an agent." I explain.

He nods and the elevator stops.

A janitorial android steps on and hits a button, standing with us. I face the flamboyant privateer now, deciding on asking for some help. "If your travels are taking you that way, I can work for passage aboard your ship."

"Well, you're a bounty hunter with obvious clearance to travel off-world for your work," He says positively, "so they must trust you. Alright, I've got room for a woman such as yourself. On two conditions, though--one, you work for your passage and two, if we pass any vessels with clearance to raid them along the way, will you assist in that raid?"

"I will." I tell him, having plenty of prior experience with combat.

He smiles and reaches out to shake my hand as the doors slide open and the android steps off. They slide shut once more and the privateer releases my hand. He turns gracefully back toward the shiny silver door. I can see his reflection in it, but what stands out most is the lip gloss. "Alright, well; once you have your mark, find me outside."

And with that, my doors slide open and I step out. I have a good feeling about this man.

13

Allun

"It's a miracle you're still alive."

I hear a woman's voice as I wake. A blinding light forces my eyes shut just as soon as I open them. My head is killing me. I continue to hear the clicking of machines around me and robotic voices going off about someone's condition (probably mine), as well as medical lingo being thrown around.

I have no idea where I am, but it's not my cell. My cell light broke a few weeks ago. Last thing I remember is guards beating the shit out of me, telling me that I've shed too much blood in their prison for them to allow it. I remember an empty room with dim red lights and being tied to a pole in the back. I remember the beating they gave me. I can still *feel* the beating they gave me. I must have blacked out after that.

I had a dream, though. In my unconscious state, I actually managed to have a dream that I remember for the first time in a long time. I was a young man again, probably just a teenage boy. Rin was there, the bitch--but it was long before she was a bitch. Long before I even had kids.

We were in the fields of pre-industrialized Tartarus. Pink leaves fell all around us from the trees surrounding the fields. Sun hit the her in such a perfect light that I actually noticed her beauty for the first time in a long time. She talked to me in such a sweet voice (although I can't remember what she said) that I felt the love I once felt for her years ago, long before our boys died.

Then she jumped right back into her bitchy tone, slapped a helmet on me and handed me a rifle. Tossed me right into a trench. All of the soldiers around me were faceless and their deaths didn't really impact me that much at all, on my side or the enemy's. I killed as liberally as I do in life, but I received no criticism. In fact, once I hit the end of the trench, I got a medal.

Then the dream ended. Just like that.

I woke up here, and now. I'm lying on a bed stiffer than the one in my cell, and I have a tube running into my nose. I open my eyes again and yawn. The light still hurts me, but not as much as it did at first. I roll over and groan, opening my eyes.

First thing I see is a pair of tits. Not a bad first sight after having the living hell beaten out of me and almost dying. I glance up at their owner and notice a human woman of all people. I don't know if I'm in the prison clinic or a legitimate hospital, but I sure as hell don't think a human doctor would be working at either one.

I rub my head and lean up, but the doctor puts her hand on my chest and lightly urges me back. I lay back against the bed and sigh, clutching my chest. My lungs hurt like hell.

"How long was I out?" I ask the woman who I'm assuming is a doctor. She's a shorter blonde girl with big brown eyes and a very serious air about her.

"Since you've been here? A week." She informs me, catching me off-guard.

I stare at her, blank-faced. "What do you mean 'since I've been here'?" I question.

She shrugs. "You were in a ship's med bay when you arrived. I'm not sure how long you've been out since you were beaten." She tells me coldly as she begins running scans on me with a hand-held medical device typically issued to humans. Tartuan doctors' scanners are far more advanced.

I look around the room and see that my hospital room blinds are closed, not that we'd need any extra light in here.

After a moment, she stops the scans. "Alright, you can sit up now."

I hoist myself upward and feel an immediate pain in my back and chest. I look down and notice my chest is bandaged up. I'm wondering how my face looks, but the mirror isn't in my immediate line of sight.

"Where am I, anyway?" It's a human world, given the architecture.

She glances over a clipboard quietly before answering me, as if she couldn't just say it and be done with it. "Earth." She tells me and I feel one of two emotions, though I can't tell which it is: intense anger or intense satisfaction. On one end, I'm out of prison. On the other, I'm on the human home world--in a hospital, no less. I'm surprised the doctors have managed to keep me alive for this long, honestly. This isn't exactly the high point of medical technology. From what I've been told, human doctors don't know shit for dick. Especially not when operating on Tartuans. I feel a sharp pain in my chest, while the tube tickles my nose.

"Allun Vortigan, is it?"

"Yeah..." I'm silent for a few minutes while she runs a couple more scans. "You got a smoke?"

"Mr. Vortigan, you've suffered severe lung damage. You can't-"

"Look, honey, I've had a really fucking rough time lately. I just need a smoke." I tell her, pulling at the tube in my nose.

She swats my hand away from it and continues her scans.

"Is that too much to ask for?"

"Well, considering it will kill you," she starts, "Yes. It is too much."

"What? Cancer?" I scoff. I'm not going to let cancer be the thing that finishes me off. Not to mention that Tartuans have already cured it.

"No, your lungs couldn't handle it. Your death would be pretty immediate." She pauses momentarily, and a beep comes in on the intercom by the door. She puts her thumb down on the button, and another loud beep rings through.

"Two men to see Mr. Allun Vortigan."

"Send them in." She turns back to me. "These guys have been coming in every day to check if you were awake. They claim to be friends of yours."

"Since when did I have friends on Earth?" I groan and stare over at operation tools.

If I need to take care of anyone, they're right there. My doctor--whose tag reads 'Doctor Schrader'--shrugs and opens up the room door.

Two rather burly gentlemen step in, both humans. They carry no expressions on their faces, and I can spot two guns in their shirt pockets, though I bet no one else here could. Maybe they're here to hit me, maybe not, but these guys are not in any legitimate business, by human standards. One of them looks to the doctor and waves her out.

She shakes her head. "I'm to tend to Mr. Vortigan-"

"We need some time alone with him. It'll be fine." One of them says in a very convincing tone.

Doctor Schrader hesitantly moves toward the door and steps out after thinking it over. Smart move on her part.

She closes the door behind her, leaving me in the care of these two obvious hired thugs. I don't blame her, though. If they're here to hit me, they'd kill her, too.

"Mr. Vortigan? My friend here and I are with the government. We're going to need to ask you some questions about-"

"What was that?" I ask falsely.

He begins to repeat himself. "We're with the government-"

"I'm sorry, I... I can't hear you on account of all of this shit that's spewing from your mouth; it's kind of muffling your words."

"Alright, look, prick," His associate blurts out, "We're here for one thing and one thing only: to get information for our boss. Now, you're gonna start telling us about the size of the Vortigan army and all of Proscriptus' weak points, or we're going to start breaking your fingers."

"I've only been to Proscriptus twice," I inform him politely, "And if you threaten me again I'm going to take that piece of yours out of your pocket and blow three holes in you; one for your cock and each ball. Then I'm going to take your arm, shove it up your buddy here's ass and turn him into a puppet. That sound good to either of you?"

"Eat shit and die, scumbag," The guy closest to me says, taking a step forward. He wears a brown duster, while his friend wears a regular suit jacket. "Now, what's the easiest entry point to Proscriptus?"

These motherfuckers just don't listen.

"You know, we're surrounded by doctors. Go out there and ask one of them about a medicine to help you get it up, so maybe then it will help you do what I'm about to ask of you: go fuck yourself." I eye the scalpels on the table beside me. My muscles are sore, but I think I can do it.

When the man reaches out to punch me, as I expected him to, I grab him by the wrist and sweep up a scalpel. I bury it into his wrist veins and he starts to bleed quick. I release his wrist and rush into his coat pocket, taking cover behind him. His friend doesn't even have time to react before I have the gun. I knock the bleeding man to the side and put a shot to man's shin. He falls screaming.

I rip the tube from my nose so I can pick myself up, ignoring the pain that comes with it. I fire blasts to disable his right shoulder, then his left.

I hear the emergency alarms ringing as I limp my way closer to him. The bastard is tough, in the sense that he hasn't fallen on his face yet. I punch him across the face and grab him by the throat. "Who hired you, eh?"

"Fuck you." He spits blood. Disgusting red human blood.

I punch him again, but this is getting nowhere. Everyone has a weak point. I can hear rushing down the hallway now.

I limp over to the door and lock it, turning back around. I see the man whose wrist I slit on the floor in a puddle of his own blood. His eyes are cold and dead. I drag myself back over to the table and pick another scalpel. I hear banging on the door now. I hold the scalpel to the wounded man's nostril and grin. He's trying not to show his fear, but I can smell it. I could smell it ten miles away.

"I can make you suffer," I say as I begin to dig the blade into the side of his nostril, "And let you survive as a living deformity, or I can let you go. Your choice."

"Cut my throat, you mean." He grunts.

I shrug. "All up to you."

It doesn't take too long into the carving to get him to talk. Blood streams down his face and he screams.

"You gonna talk?"

The banging on the door is getting louder. Shouts are coming from the other side. Security is pissed.

"A politician!" He yelps. "A politician named Chandler Bloomfield!"

"Why does Chandler Bloomfield give a shit?"

"H-He wants war with the Vortigans!" He lets out a pained scream of the obvious.

"I got that much, dipshit."

"He wants a war with the Vortigans so he can make money off of the industry!"

I will admit it, war is very profitable. However, this Chandler Bloomfield made a mistake. I've said it before and I'll say it again. The name Vortigan is not a fucking joke. It could have been anyone. He could have waged war on anyone in the galaxy and he's using his armies against the Vortigans. "When is he planning on attacking Proscriptus?" I demand.

He shrugs. "I-I don't know! I don't know!"

He's lying. He's given away enough already, he doesn't want to give away anymore. However, customer-criminal confidentiality doesn't stand up so well when a man is being dug into with a scalpel. "Yes you fucking do!" I start carving more slowly.

He hisses and squeals. "Two months! Two months!"

"Good man." He's telling the truth now.

I rip the scalpel from his bloody face and step out of the way. He falls to the floor screeching. I drop the scalpel and move toward the door, human blood all over my hands. I slide the lock and open up the door, weary and sore. I fall onto my back, taking a deep breath. The pain is just now getting back to me.

Security guards rush me, and nurses hoist me back up onto the bed as I start to fall under again. I'm not quite unconscious, though. I can make out what's happening around me. "Did none of you bastards think to get a key?" I laugh, looking down at the dead man beside my bed.

"They weren't working. Somebody jammed the lock."

"Probably the same fuckers who just tried to kill me."

The man living one groans and weeps like a widow. I chuckle at the sound of it. "Hey, calm down. We're in a hospital. What better place to be wounded?"

14

Praxis

"Runnin' down to Cuba with a load of sugar! Weigh me boys to Cuba! Make her run, you lime-juice squeezers! Runnin' down to Cuba!"

I've always loved the cheerful songs of spacers. I've never been on a ship with privateers until lately, but they're even more fun from what I've seen.

It's been two weeks since I departed from Alkineth and said goodbye to Cal, Calypso, Aeson and their children. They seemed both sad and relieved to see me go. I came off as dangerous during my entire stay, so it was no wonder that they were relieved that I was leaving.

Aeson was the only one who seemed to remain easy around me because, like me, he was a trained killer. After our goodbyes, I found myself hopping aboard a pirate's vessel. I've been doing work as the first mate's assistant and I have to say, this man is gorgeous.

He's a Delkyrian who's actually native to Seregua and bears a pair of big white wings, as opposed to the usual Delkyrian black and brown. His horns spiral like a ram's and he's rarely caught wearing anything but pants and a red bandanna wrapped around his forehead, soaked in the blood of soldiers he fought in some big Delkyrain clan war. He has long blonde hair that he typically puts up in a ponytail and often carries a sword with the emblem of his clan in the scabbard on his belt. I follow behind him when he needs me, but that isn't often. Still, it's the work I do for my passage aboard the ship.

The first mate, Jeth'ro, requested it himself. I sit in his office, waiting for him to finish marking down numbers for the ship treasury in a book on his desk. He eventually finishes writing it down and looks up to me. His big red eyes graze over me and pass on to stare at a picture of some stone castle from his home city on Seregua.

"So my captain tells me you are headed to Seregua, no?" His accent is a bit broken, but I can still make out what he says. He smiles at me and lays down his pen, standing up. He turns to a chest beside the chair I sit in and heads over to it. He swings open the top of the trunk and begins digging around.

"Yes sir." I tell him, nodding.

He grins and hoists up a sword, stuck in a scabbard and wrapped in cloth. Something he just had laying around, so probably not anything high quality. He lays it on his desk and sighs, stepping around the room lightly. "Have you ever been to Seregua, my dear?"

He calls me that as a term of endearment, though I'm not sure if he understands the typical context of the statement. I've mostly seen it in a romantic sense and he, despite having me serving under him by choice, has not shown any romantic interest in me.

"Can't say I have." I say, looking to the picture. The keep is old and beautiful, with trees growing through it and vines growing on its walls. If most of the architecture on Seregua looks like this, I'd be glad to pay it more visits. "Is it beautiful?"

"She is my motherland," He tells me, "And she is the most astonishing thing in this galaxy. Her trees grow higher than the tallest skyscraper and her children, the Delkyrians and all of our bestial companions on the world, have grown wiser with age due to her teachings. She is the mother to all her children. If only they would not shed so much of their own blood."

His emotions for the world are genuine and very present. He begins unfolding the cloth, looking to me in expectation. "And if you are to reach anyone in my motherland, you must wield a sword. Blasters are not forbidden, but they are a coward's weapon when in presence of sword fighters. And you, Praxis, do not seem to be a coward."

"I don't really know *how* to use a sword." I tell him, but he only gives a knowing smirk.

He pulls the blade from the scabbard to reveal a shining silver-like metal, although it's much sturdier than silver. It's what most Delkyrian blades are forged from. He gently hands it over to me and I inspect it. It holds his clan's emblem. Probably an older blade from when he was young. "I will teach you, Praxis," He says as he reaches for the scabbard.

He tosses it to me, and I lay the sword down on top of the chest beside me, looping the scabbard to my belt. Once it's secure, I slide the sword in and stand from the chair. His office doors swing open and he immediately begins leading me, most likely to the combat deck. The man is beautiful and charismatic, making me feel almost like I don't have a chance with him--not that it would affect me much if I didn't, but still. "I will show you the ways of a Delkyrian swordsman."

"Why are you so liberal with your teachings?" I ask him, causing him to grin.

"You are beautiful," He sighs, "And beauty is a trait I most admire. It would be quite the waste if you were bested and slain, especially on my own beautiful home-world. The last thing she needs is more blood on her soil, just as it is the last thing *you* need is to have your blood spilled."

He takes me to the training deck and looks around. Inside the training deck is a large window made of unbreakable glass that overlooks space. I can see another red star. They're gorgeous.

I look around at various members of the privateer who calls himself Golden Tom's crew crossing blades and firing training blasters. Jeth'ro looks around to see about who he might bring over. He spots two men crossing blades on the far side of the room and his dark red eyes light up. "Miguel! Ryder!" He yelps and the two come barreling over, their training blades in hand. "Toss our new friend Praxis here a training blade and let me see how she stands against the two of you."

"Yes sir!"

The one known as Ryder takes a sprint toward the training swords on a rack. Ryder is a bit young to be a privateer, in my opinion, but I was a hit-man when I was around his age, so what does it matter? Miguel seems about the same age and I've seen them both around the crew, usually together. They're inseparable. Ryder tosses me a blade and takes a stance as Jeth'ro begins his role as a teacher.

"Now, Praxis, show me how you defend. Miguel, Ryder, attack."

They charge at me headfirst, training blades swinging.

I manage to knock one out of the way, but the other hits me right in the gut. I don't double over, though. I've taken harder hits.

Jeth'ro shakes his head and holds up his hand, extending his large white wings for a moment, flapping them and then pulling them back in to himself. "No, no, dear. You stand like you're holding a blaster to the back of a man's head and you swing like an old woman with a cane. Turn to your side."

I turn and immediately notice the benefit. I'm a harder target now.

"If you... If you weren't so voluptuous in the chest area, perhaps you would be harder to hit as a whole. But still, you're thin enough everywhere else that you're not going to be too easy to hit." He complimented my breasts.

I wonder whether or not that was intentional. "*Voluptuous*, eh?" I laugh and he winks, but immediately goes back to his teaching mode. "You mentioned my swing?"

"Yes, um... You swing, as I say, like an old woman. You need to sting. You need to strike like a scorpion, move your body like a cat and run your feet like a rabbit. You other races, though, you do not fight like the Delkyrians. You cannot slow time in your own eyes and give yourself the advantage. You must pay close attention quickly and keep your enemy off of you. Swing with circular wrist motions. Sweep their legs, their side, their arms; their throat, if you can. You may not move like my people, you may not think like my people, but I can give you one thing: I can help you move with the grace and care of my people."

"Maybe you should show me firsthand the 'movements of your people.'" I flirt, forgetting about the crewmen surrounding us.

Jeth'ro smiles and nods. "Perhaps when training is done." He tells me. "Miguel, Ryder, back to the action. I want to see Praxis move now."

* * * *

I feel Jeth'ro's body over my own under his cabin bed sheets. Our lips lock and I drag my nails down his back with one hand, pulling his ponytail with the other. It's the only thing I can do to steady myself as the bed rattles.

After some moaning, some sweating and some unfurled wings, he collapses beside me. He rolls over onto his back and takes a long, deep breath. He rolls over and puts his head on my chest, wrapping his arm around my waist.

The room is quiet and dark, but our breathing can still be heard quite clearly. His port window reveals the void of space and I can see the mottled stars in the sky outside of it. I take a breath and smile, putting my own arms around Jeth'ro. It was a lovely event. Maybe he'll start letting me sleep in here more often.

"Praxis?" He reaches back and pulls off his ponytail holder, letting his long hair drop past his shoulders. It was a mess anyway. He looks up at me and I can see his red eyes in through the darkness. "You are absolutely beautiful."

"So are you." I tell him, without informing him that his horn is poking me in the boob. It doesn't bother me that much and his horns are dulled anyway, so I don't kill the moment.

"The moment I saw you aboard this ship, I... I recognized that beauty. That is why I requested your presence beside me." He tells me, "Although your personality has also proven to be quite attractive just as well."

"I hope you don't expect anything long-term." I break the news to him, but I can't see his expression through the darkness.

After a moment, he speaks up. "I do not. We have our separate paths. You travel the road of a hunter and I travel the road of a pirate. Paths will often change and intertwine; I do hope, though, that our paths may cross again after you leave this ship. Until then, I am willing to train with you, make love to you and provide you with company if you'd like. If not, I will repeat: we go our separate paths."

"Jeth'ro," I tell him with a grin, "I will train with you and I will make love to you as often as I can from tonight until the night I leave." I lean down and give him a peck on the lips, rubbing his head and running my fingers through his smooth, soft hair.

He makes a satisfied sigh, and the red in his eyes disappears from the room as his eyelids shut. He moves his head back up to his pillow and rolls over. I roll to him and wrap my arm over him, pressing myself against his back. This voyage is going to be pretty nice. I can just tell.

* * * *

The alarms ring through the halls of the ship and into the dark room that I lie in. Jeth'ro is already up far faster than I am, quickly rushing for the light switch. The lights appear all throughout the room, blinding me momentarily.

Once my eyes become adjusted, I pick myself up out of the bed to see Jeth'ro throwing on his pants and blood-stained bandanna. He loops his blade's sheath to his belt and immediately breaks for the door. I begin tossing on my clothes as well and grab one of Jeth'ro's sidearms. I stuff the pistol into the holster on my belt and make for the door after him. He's already out of sight by the time I enter the dimly lit hall, although I don't quite know where he's gone.

Crewmen rush by me, swords and guns at the ready. I see Miguel and Ryder running one right after the other, cutting around me and sprinting. I pass a large Undrian with a blaster rifle sized to fit his hands hanging from his shoulder by a strap, grunting. His footsteps echo through the hall, his feet crashing again and again against the cold hard floor. I follow the Undrian, who is the easiest to keep up with. The alarms still ring, paining the ears of likely everyone on the crew who isn't deaf.

Eventually the alarms cut and the Welsh accent of Captain Golden Tom takes over. "This ship isn't your average one, boys. This is Rogue Agency coming at us. Their guns aren't trained on us, but ready yourselves to fight. Engineers, steady yourselves and get on the cannons. The rest of you, prepare to board. I'll do the talking."

I continue to follow the Undrian until he reaches the entrance tube. The entrance tube is designed to extend from one ship to another, either through puncturing a hole in the side of the ship and entering by force or aligning it to another ship's door and going through on good terms.

Waiting with the Undrian and I are probably eighty or so men and women, packed together with rifles, pistols and swords at their belts or in their hands. The room is wide enough to hold us all without any struggle, at least.

Eventually, the intercom system comes on again and the voice of Tom grabs our attention once more. "They claim to be friendly. They're RA, so I'm not taking the chance. We're letting them on. They're extending their tube to our door."

"Great," the Undrian groans. "Just what we need. A bunch of Rogue Agency fucks coming onto our ship and telling us how to operate."

* * * *

The Rogue Agency called for me.

I stand on the bridge of the ship and face five men in black, all Rogue Agency. Golden Tom sits in his captain's chair and looks them over, his hand on his chin; Jeth'ro stands loyally beside him. An extraordinarily large blaster, modeled after a flintlock pistol, lies across Tom's lap. Floral patterns cover the top of the barrel and the actual gun itself seems to be encased in more aesthetically themed parts, such as a wooden stock. The barrel is shining and golden, matching Tom's makeup. His hand is off of the gun, but it is present.

The Rogue Agency men look around the bridge suspiciously before seeing me. I step out of the elevator and up to a navigator's mapping table that's located in the center of the room.

"Praxis?" A Tartuan man with a medal on his chest asks, stepping up to the table across from me. "Former Vortigan Justicar?"

"That would be me." I say, immediately hatching a plan to kill all five if it comes to it.

The Tartuan places his hands on the table and leans forward, smiling at me. Not a suspicious or malicious smile; just a smile. "What does the Rogue Agency need from me?"

"We're not here to demand anything." He says, reaching out to shake my hand. I reluctantly accept the gesture. "We're here to ask if you will so kindly join us."

"Why would I join you?" I ask, pulling my hand back.

He turns to stare out of the port, into open space. I can see the tail end of their large warship even from here. He sighs before turning back to me. "Because you could get the chance to go out there and fly. You could do anything, liberate worlds, save lives, stop wars; the choice would be yours."

"Recruits don't get to make choices." I retort, "and I'm not interested in joining a military."

"We're not a military." He tries to correct, but I remain unconvinced. They wear uniforms, they follow regulations, they're trained in a specific way and they live for combat; if that's not a military, I don't know what is. "And besides, you wouldn't *be* a recruit! Do you think we'd pull over this ship and go out of our way to find you if we wanted to put you in the shoes of an ensign? If we wanted recruits, we'd stop at the nearest backwater world and start handing out fliers to their youth. What I'm talking about here is a captain deal! Think about it! Rogue Agency First Commander Praxis. Sounds sweet, doesn't it?"

"We're done here." I say, turning back to the elevator.

I manage to take a few steps, but his words beckon me back. "You're an invasion-era Alkin. You know what war does to people and worlds. Why don't you join us and help prevent wars?" He asks me, but his attempt at inspiration only manages to offend.

"I don't want to prevent wars," I storm back over to the table. My boots clap against the hard metal floor as I approach. "I want to avoid them. I want nothing to do with them."

"Even when your home is involved?" He asks.

I immediately feel sick. I don't know which home he's referring to, whether it be Alkineth or Proscriptus, but I know that I'm not going to like the sound of his next statement.

"I didn't want to drop the ball so soon, but I need captains for the sake of the Vortigans. Proscriptus is in danger and I need ships. To have good ships, I need good captains. Allun Vortigan called me a while back and recommended you as a captain to me. So will you captain one of my ships, even if temporarily?"

"How do you know Allun?" I ask. He grins.

"Best friends since childhood. I didn't introduce myself, did I? Rogue Agency Fleet Admiral Pairus. He never mentioned me?"

"I didn't spend enough time around him before he got arrested for him to."

I can't read any lies in this guy's statements. Proscriptus may very well be in trouble. The last thing I want is the destruction of the place I spent a good portion of my life, as well as the destruction of the people I spent it with. "Anyway, maybe I'll take you up on your offer. I've got a condition, though: when Proscriptus is safe, I can walk out any time."

"Deal." He says, reaching out to shake my hand again. "But if you find it to your liking, I'd appreciate it if you kept the ship."

"You need ships, eh?" Tom asks, standing upright. He slides the blaster into a holster strapped to his back, due to it being too large to hold on his hip. "And if a ship were offered to you, how much would you pay?"

"I have eight-point-five million I can spare overall. If your ship and crew are worth a damn, I can pay you eighty-thousand once the battle is done."

Tom's eyes light up and a smile stretches across his face. "Right, then!" He cheers, "And how many ships are we going up against?"

"Anywhere between four-hundred and six-hundred. So far, we have five-hundred."

"I've been in worse scraps." Tom states, turning to his intercom microphone. He holds down the button and opens up his mouth to speak. *"Attention, dear crew! We are joining a defense! Eighty-thousand split between us and whatever we can get from the ships we destroy!"*

15

Allun

Chandler Bloomfield is the very definition of a rich prick. Like many men of his political profession, he owns an army, a fleet and a mentally poisoned crowd of supporters. He exists to manipulate, steal and kill. He is racist. He is hateful.

More than anything, I've learned, is that he knows how much money a war with the Vortigans can make him. We are not exactly idolized within human society and are often seen as legal criminals, like many Tartuan families. Chandler Bloomfield furthers this idea that we are lawless, Godless bastards. Godless, maybe. Lawless? Not a fucking chance. There have been only a handful of anarchist Vortigans in the past, my youngest son included, and they're all dead.

Chandler Bloomfield doesn't like to admit that to his supporters, though. He's gained independence from the government's restraints and had a law passed that allowed him and his like-minded sheep to declare war in their own name rather than that of the Human Empire.

After gaining this knowledge through spending time on Earth, due to the fact that Chandler Bloomfield has kept his policies on Earth and not allowed any of his plans to leave, I made a call to my good friend Pairus. Now, my job in this is done. I am bored to tears.

Doctor Schrader has been my only company so far. She stands with an android at her back, on the far side of the room. She deposits medicine into a machine that's supposed to distribute it to me in the proper doses at the proper times. I think about how I should be on Proscriptus right now getting ready to blow a bunch of human invaders to Hell, but thinking about it does me no good. Instead of shooting, I'm getting shots and having pills administered into my system daily.

"So, doc," I say in a monotone voice. The pills have temporarily killed most of the excitement in my head, and now I'm talking like an early-model robot. "You wanna go out to dinner sometime?"

"You're not permitted to leave the hospital." She states brusquely.

I sigh and lay down in my bed, pulling the sheets over me.

"And besides, I'd be chastised by everyone if I went out with a Tartuan."

"That's right. Ain't that illegal here?" I ask.

She shakes her head. "The relationship between one alien race and another? No. The marriage? Absolutely."

"That's some discriminatory rakia shit." I groan.

She nods. "Yeah, I know. It's a shame, too. I could see myself marrying a Delkyrian, maybe, or one of those Sprites that have been coming to Earth lately."

"Y' know, I've never been with a human before." I tell her, but she brushes it off.

"Maybe you will someday."

"Gets pretty lonely in this hospital room." I begin to flirt, but she shuts me down immediately.

I wish that previous statement were just me being a lying scumbag, but it really is lonely. I have no one to talk to, and I have a limited number of calls I can make in a day. The last person I talked to on the phone was Alex and that was weeks ago. All we talked about was the assault that was to come, because I was warning him. The doctors still won't let me leave the hospital, the nurses and doctors all turn me down when I hit on them, none of them have time to talk outside of my flirtations and the other patients are all brain-dead or racist and the chef in the cafeteria is a mute.

"No." Schrader growls. "I'm not sleeping with you."

"I didn't expect you would." I sigh, rolling on my side and staring out of the open blinds. I can see ships flying back and forth in the sky and people walking around the streets in the distance. "Is prostitution legal here?"

"There are no prostitutes in the hospital."

"No active ones, maybe, but I'm pretty sure I saw some off-duty in the cafeteria."

"Allun, I know it sucks being cooped up in here, but can you handle being bored and *not* annoying me?"

"Ah, fuck you." I growl. "It's these damn pills fucking with my head. You got any smokes?"

She remains quiet, finishing her work and leaving the room with the android at her back.

I turn on the TV and stare blankly at human news. They talk about Sprite immigration, gun policy, piracy and interracial marriage. I groan and close my eyes, trying to get some sleep. I can't even sleep. I just lie in my bed, mentally deceased and so bored I almost feel like I'm in purgatory.

* * * *

That's it. It's been eight hours since Schrader left, and I've had no one to talk to since. I didn't take my medicine when I was supposed to and I don't need to. I know that Doctor Schrader is off now, and she's been working with me exclusively. Maybe the other workers won't notice me or realize that I don't have clearance to leave if I start to walk out. If they do, I'll tell them to fuck off. Security tries to get involved, I'll knock them on their asses.

I can see the city lights outside my window, and they're shimmering like the goddamn stars. Since I haven't been taking my medicine, my vision is starting to get blurry. I'm starting to feel dizzy and tired, but I'm bored and I can't sleep.

I hoist myself up and move toward the door with a sense of purpose. I am leaving this damned hospital. I am making my way out of here, no matter what. I've been here for weeks. I've been following the same routine, day after day, week after week. I've lost track of the time. Every day is living hell.

I swing the door open and clap my feet against the marble floor. I step over each crack in a pattern, which is something I've used to entertain myself and made a habit of here; it's a small form of entertainment, if you can call it that, but it's better than nothing.

I see the nurses behind the counter chattering. I lighten my steps, and they don't notice me. I slip past them and make my way to the elevators. The elevator stops, and an android steps in. He scans my face and starts to make me nervous, so I rip the cord on his neck and turn his ass off. He collapses face-forward with a *clank*.

I keep moving ahead, ignoring the robot I just brought down. The elevator stops at the ground floor.

I walk to the front door and take a deep breath. No one has noticed me so far. The security guards are paying me no mind, so I slide the door open and step out into the space just before the outside. I can feel the heat pouring down on me now. I can hardly breathe, but I manage to force the next door open.

The heat slams against me like a brick to the head. The fresh air is nice--far too nice for me to breathe in right after an eternity in a place that smells like medicine, bleach, ass and death. I manage to make it just across the street before I feel like collapsing.

I keep on moving. I'm not falling. I'm finding something. A night club, a musty dive, a brothel, a cafe`... I don't care what it is as long as it's not that hospital.

The heat reminds me of home, back in Tartarus. The trees here are beautiful and flourishing. I can see a park just down the road. Maybe I'll go there and lay in the grass, look at the stars. I can see a man and a woman sitting on a bench conversing. Conversation sounds nice; too bad I'm too exhausted to have one.

I feel my torso getting heavier and heavier as I drag myself forward. I'm halfway across the road and the light is about to change. I can feel it coming. I begin moving faster, but my sprint turns to a stumble.

I fall onto the sidewalk and catch myself with my hands. The strain on my arms is too much so I release. I roll to my side and pant, pulling my legs up onto the sidewalk with my arms. It hurts to move them anymore. My limbs feel limp and lifeless. I can move them, but at the cost of pain in my muscles and very bones.

"Sir?" I hear the woman on the bench say and footsteps patter toward me. Light ones followed by heavy. I look to my right and see the man and woman both heading for me. "Sir, do you need to go to the hospital?"

"Take me back there and I bite your goddamn fingers off!" I bark at them between breaths, rolling onto my stomach and dragging myself with my arms. I'm doing it, damn it. I'm making it to that grass. "You want to help me, help me get to the grass."

That grass. Sweet salvation, that grass. Something that isn't cold and hard. Something I can get behind. Something that makes me feel alive.

"Sir, you're... You need to go to the hospital."

"I will break your legs if you take me back there!"

I can feel my hands on the grass. I pull myself a little further forward. I think my legs may have quit working entirely. This grass is soft and prickly. I haven't felt grass against my skin since my time in the army.

I groan; my chest makes it onto the grass. I go even further until my knees hit. My right arm craps out on me. Left arm, you're my last chance here. I use all my might to drag myself onward.

My feet hit the ground, and I stop pulling myself. I roll over my arm and onto my back. My body is twisted. I can't move a damn thing anymore except my head. But I can see the stars. If only I knew which direction Tartarus is.

16

Praxis

"Settling in, Captain Praxis?"

Alex steps in with a cigar in his mouth. He wears a tucked-in button-down, suspenders and black slacks. His beard is grown out again, longer than before.

I stand on the bridge of my ship with pilots, navigators and other technicians all around me. They wear black uniforms, but not suits. These uniforms are one-piece jumpsuits with patches on them; most of them customized but the name of each technician written on a patch across the chest.

I, myself, have a captain's uniform: a black space captain's hat with a trim of golden leaves in the front and the words 'Rogue Agency' written in the center, a white button-down, a black tie and a black suit-jacket over it; to top it all off, I have a black skirt that comes to my knees.

"Don't get used to calling me that." I brush him off, sitting down in my captain's seat without even realizing it. Jeth'ro and Golden Tom have two fold-out seats across from me, seeing as this is a meeting to discuss the defense of Proscriptus. Pairus leans back against the wall in the corner and nods to Alex, grinning. "I only plan on captaining until the defense is done."

"We'll see." Alex says and looks to Pairus, grinning back. "Pairus, you old bastard, come here!"

Pairus runs forward and grabs Alex and gives him a hug tighter than a bear trap. He lifts up, and I can see Alex's feet leaving the ground. Pairus spins with Alex, still holding the hug, and then sits him back down.

"Now, on to business," Alex says, getting rid of the creases in his shirt and pants. He straightens his suspenders and puts his hands in his pockets, standing beside my captain's chair. "We've got a war coming up."

"Not a war," Pairus corrects him. "If it were a war, I'd have failed at doing my job. We've got a battle coming. I have no idea where the fleet is, but once it reaches us, we're going to destroy it. Once it's destroyed, one of us in the Rogue Agency is going to have to make Chandler Bloomfield disappear. It's going to be me or one of my captains..." He looks to me in anticipation, as if I'm obligated to do it. "Praxis?"

"As good as I am at making people disappear," I jest, "I don't plan on sticking around that long."

"Come on; take him onto your ship and dish out *your* justice, then once it's done if you don't want to be a captain, you can go."

He drives a hard bargain. Despite not being a part of the Vortigans anymore, I do still feel responsible for Proscriptus and I do want to kill anyone that gets in the way of defending it.

I sigh, shaking my head. He drives a hard bargain. "Alright." I submit. "I'll get rid of the bastard, but on to business. We need a defense."

"I've been thinking on this." Pairus holds up his hand to halt anyone else from speaking before him. "Now I have five-hundred ships in my fleet, plus Captain Tom's ship to make five-hundred-and-one.

Only problem is that only four-fifty of the ships in my fleet are operational, either due to engineering issues or lack of captains to command them. Two-hundred can be here within the week, but they're a strong two-hundred. If the ships don't show up by next week, we can get two-hundred more. For now, we're going to have to work with our two-hundred-and-one. Tom and Praxis, I want the two of you by the docks. I'll send twelve ships to aid you. I want the two of you to fight off any ships that come near the docks. If I give the signal, I want you to dock and form a line of defense inside of Proscriptus itself.

"Alex, I want you to round up all of the Vortigan ships you can. I'd like the number to be in the hundreds, but I'll take what I can get. Tom, do you have any pirate friends we might be able to convince to join this fight?"

"*Privateer* friends." Tom corrects, waving a finger. "And I'll see if Barry the Bludgeon or Toothless Edward's crews can join."

I try my best not to ask *why* they carry these nicknames. It's hard to resist asking, though. If a spacer has a nickname, there's more to it than what it sounds like. I'm going to go out on a limb and say Toothless Edward probably isn't toothless. More than likely, he rips teeth out of his victims' mouths or something of the sort. "Hey Tom, anyone ever tell you you've got a sing-song voice?"

"You ever been to Wales?" Tom asks, leaning back and lighting a cigar.

Alex shrugs. "Is it on Earth?" Alex asks cynically.

"Yep."

"Then fuck no I've never been to Wales. You ever been to Sar Vort?" Alex asks, to which Tom nods.

"I have. You bastards always sound like you're coughing up shit when you speak. It's like you've been eating sandpaper." Golden Tom prods at Alex, who just smiles in return.

"Alright, I'll give you that one." Alex ends the dialogue by turning back toward Pairus and paying mind to the planning.

The planning goes on and on until we've marked a spot for every ship we might have and every soldier we do. Pairus dispatches a few stealth vessels to scout ahead and the meeting is adjourned. I find myself sitting on my ship with Golden Tom, Jeth'ro and Alex without anything for the rest of us to do.

Alex proposes we get a drink, so we all head down the elevator and into my new ship's crew bar. I still haven't finished exploring the damn thing. *Wait, it's not my ship*, I have to remind myself. *I'm just using it. Once this is over, I'm dropping it.*

* * * *

I follow three young characters on the TV in my old Proscriptus penthouse. Tom, Alex and Jeth'ro all sit with me on the old sofa and watch along.

Our eyes are all trained on a movie that Tom recommended. The three figures are all human, two young Irishmen and a Welshman. The Welsh boy looks just like Tom--*just* like him. A younger incarnation, perhaps, but his motions, his looks and his manner of speaking are Golden Tom to a T. He's even Welsh.

Alex and I both look to Tom, but he continues watching with Jeth'ro. He doesn't acknowledge our stares, so we turn back to the TV and watch.

"Boys," Tom's voice echoes through the speakers. *"It's been a pleasure."* His character shakes hands with both of the Irishmen, hopping onto the back of a horse and riding off into the distance. The Irishmen turn their backs on the camera, walking down the road on a separate path. The credits roll and we turn to Tom again.

Tom sighs and turns to the rest of us, finally. "So...?" He asks for an opinion, but none of us seemed to pay any attention to the movie itself.

Alex sinks into his seat. "So you're an actor?"

"I am a privateer." Tom growls. "I *used* to be an actor."

"So what happened?" Alex pries further into Tom's past.

"Well acting wasn't paying the bills after my younger sister got the Astarian Plague. I... I don't know how it happened. It's so rare for non-Astarians to get it. I needed to do something to make more money. I sought a trainer, became a marksman, a swordsman and a martial artist and I took to the stars. It was legal piracy. Kill, steal, pillage--but it was good money. It was in vain, though. She died, despite the money I paid for her treatment. I founded a charity with the rest. Now, the majority of my share of the money we make from privateering goes to not only the research of a cure for Astarian Plague, but for all diseases that ail us."

"Jesus." Alex stands and starts to head for the kitchen. "I can't lie and say I know how it feels. Nobody in my family has ever died from disease. It's always been blaster wounds or slit throats. Still, you have my sympathies. Most people wouldn't turn directly to privateering, though. What made you do it?"

"Honestly? It... It was partly for myself. Ever since I was a kid, I always wanted to be a pirate. Since I've gotten older, I've realized that there's no point in piracy when you can be a privateer and legally get away with the same things a pirate would be executed for."

"That's kind of fucked." Alex laughs. "But hey, who am I to judge?"

17

Allun

The hospital room they moved me to is dingy. It's cold, cramped and cluttered with barely any viewing range out into the world. I much preferred the prison cell. At least in there I had somebody to talk to.

Since my attempt to spring free from this living Hell, not even Doctor Schrader talks to me anymore. She isn't even my primary doctor now. The only doctors that have been coming to see me have been androids that fumble with the machines I'm hooked to every once in a while, and they can't even talk.

My arms and legs don't work, haven't ever since I tried to spring loose. Doctor Schrader said that they got me hooked up quick enough that they can still save my limbs, if I don't try rolling off the bed or anything. Tubes are still running into my nose, my ears and even my ass now. It's one of the most unpleasant things I've ever felt, having cold tubes shoved everywhere but my mouth and my cock hole.

A little spider android clacks its feet against the floor as it circles the room, checking machine after machine. I stare blankly at a TV screen. I can't even change the channel, and all that's on is an evangelical preacher screaming about the end times. I can hear his psychotic wailing all around the room. The speakers make it echo, as if his voice isn't hard enough to hear without having to hear it projected.

I hear the beeping of the intercom. *"Allun Vortigan, you have a visitor."*

As if I could fucking answer that machine. I get no say in who comes to visit me. It's probably another assassin or the like. Despite the need for double security around my door, this wing of the hospital gives me less.

Not that it matters, of course, because a man like Chandler Bloomfield can get into anywhere using just his name. Hell, his maid probably uses his name to get into places free of charge or penalty. The man could own worlds if he tried; he aims to, if this war with the Vortigans works out for him.

I know plenty about him now, after doing some research on the one computer I was provided in my previous room. I was never tech savvy, but it's a good idea to learn about your enemies if you can. He's an anti-Tartuan bigot, a hero to certain backwater colonies and an ultra-conservative to the point that only straight, theistic humans are allowed in the ranks of his armies and, believe me, he *does* have armies.

Not much on an imperial scale, but as far as personal armies go, this man's militia is nothing to scoff at. The thing is, if he wins this battle with Proscriptus the other human nationals are going to see this as an opportunity to take territory as well, and they're going to join in. They're going to throw everything they've got at the Vortigans, and there's going to be far more bloodshed than even a war with the Dreadwals would have caused.

Hell, the Dreadwals may rally to his side to bring us down as well. They're probably the reason I'm on Earth in the first place. Chandler Bloomfield is our ultimate enemy, and we've just now realized it.

And, speak of the Devil, here comes Chandler Bloomfield.

The door opens, I can see light break through, something I don't get much of in this compact cargo-crate of a room. I recognize his malicious smirk that he held in every picture of him I found on the internet. His short brown hair is slicked back and perfectly combed, his lifeless blue eyes scanning me and the room around me, as well as the spider android. His blue suit and red tie seem to go well together, despite appearing quite opposite to one-another. He carries no weapons that I can see, not even a knife in his pocket. Two of his soldiers stand behind him, both wearing the Bloomfield Rose pinned over their hearts.

Chandler's clean-shaven chin tilts slightly upward, along with his nose. He naturally holds it high. I build up saliva in my dry mouth and wait for an opportunity to spit in his face. The man opens his mouth to speak, but appears to take a deep breath before he can convey any words. It's as if he's so stupid he's forgotten to breathe.

"Mr. Allun Vortigan?"

His voice is higher than I expected it to be. It's high and nasally, making it sound worse than the evangelical pastor on TV. I stare, not necessarily glaring at him but not giving him the courtesy of a smile. I don't want him to think he's provoked emotion in me one way or the other. "I don't know if you know who I am, I mean, we've never met in person but we do hold a heavy impact on each other."

"Speak for yourself." I state, my look demanding he leave.

He's obviously made uncomfortable by my presence, despite *him* being the one who came here to see *me*. I inhale deeply and shake my head.

"Mr. Vortigan, I am holding your family at gunpoint here." He demands a response, but I give him none. "My armies are on the move to take your brother's space station. I can spare your brother's life if you'll cooperate with me."

"You assume he's going to lose?" I ask rhetorically. "Look, my brother's a bastard. He killed my son. He's a piece of shit and I never want to see him again; that being said, I love my brother and I will tell you something outright: he has never lost a battle. My brother's been in charge of our men for a long time. He led charges in the fucking Tecorian War. Never lost a fight. I hope I get to see the look on your face when he fucks you up so bad that your mother can feel it."

"Mr. Vortigan, you underestimate the size of my army and the abilities of my men." He's not even focusing on his original intentions now. He's just trying to convince me that he can win this pissing contest.

"And you underestimate ours. Even if you take Proscriptus, we've got whole families at our backs. Tennus, Dreadwal, Taiwarin, Jorjus-"

"I think you're bluffing." He calls me out. "The Dreadwals have far more allies than you and I have the Dreadwals in my pocket."

"Do you now?" I start to smirk.

This dumb bastard is really falling for the pissing contest manipulation tactic. He starts trying to convince me that he's got more power, he reveals far more to me than he probably should. If he doesn't kill me, he's really taking a chance. "The Dreadwals are the ones that sold you to me. However, you were a little beaten up, so we had to put you in the hospital. Otherwise, we would have been having this conversation a lot sooner." He informs me.

I feign shock. "Really? Which Dreadwals?"

"I don't know, their names are all so similar... The two boys." He says as if it doesn't make a difference. It makes a huge difference to the boys, to him, to the family. If I know who sold me, I can have them eliminated if I can get in touch with Pairus. That also means that I can scare the other families into backing us. They might start paying us tribute to keep us off their backs. I imagine that anyone with the idea to conspire against us will start thinking twice once they know we can make our enemies--no matter how dignified and important--disappear.

"But now, Mr. Vortigan, I need you to negotiate with your family. If they surrender Sar Vort after we take Proscriptus, they get you back and we let them continue to live out the rest of their lives as ordinary citizens. They're going to need your word on that. What reason have they to trust me?"

"You're irrational." I tell him in a matter-of-fact way.

He sighs and groans, whining like a baby. "Mr. Vortigan, you don't understand. If I have to take Sar Vort, I will have to kill your family. Your mother, your brothers, your sisters, your wife, kids--"

"My wife just died," I growl. "And my kids died years ago. You want my cooperation? Alright. I'll tell you what you can do to help you win the war: go purchase a revolver, load a round into the chamber, press it to the roof of your mouth and pull the trigger. You won't lose if you never compete."

"Mr. Vortigan, I tried being reasonable." He tells me.

I nod. "Your reasoning sounds pretty ridiculous, if you ask me." I smile and point with my head to the chair by my bedside. "Go on, sit down. We'll talk this out."

He does as I ask, taking a seat hesitantly.

I ready my saliva, making sure it's built up, and spit it into his face.

He wipes the wet, bubbly spit from his face and grunts, being thrown into a fit of rage. "You bastard!" He yells, "I'm going to kill you!"

"Then do it." I tell him. "What better time than now? My limbs don't work and I'm hooked to a machine."

He takes this as a challenge. He points to me and nods to his soldiers. They aim their guns for my bed, but he doesn't give them the signal to fire. This man is a bitch. This man does not know how to play his cards. This man only ever reached power because of his money and exploiting xenophobia and eugenics. How a man of his childlike pride and mindset ever came to power, I do not know.

"That's the problem with guys like you. You always have thugs do your work for you. You hire men to do your thinking for you. If anyone criticizes or insults you, you brand them an idiot or an enemy of the state and you shut yourself off from them, still dwelling in your own little world, ignorant and closed-minded. The universe isn't so black and white."

"You want me to do it myself?" He snaps. "Fine."

He walks with a sense of righteousness over to my machine, placing his hand on the cord and ripping it out.

I can feel one of the tubes stop pumping fluids into my body.

He rips another.

Then another.

He starts ripping every cord he can until there's nothing plugged into the wall anymore. I can feel my consciousness starting to fade.

"Come on." He orders his soldiers. "This man isn't going to be of any use to us anymore."

18

Praxis

Space is big. Space is terrifying.

Space is a place that I used to believe we should never really venture out into, when I was younger. Space holds far too many secrets, I thought. I always believed it would be unexplorable.

As it happens, nothing is unexplorable. Not space, not the sea, no world and no life. I plan on exploring my mind. My consciousness. My being. I'm going to give this Rogue Agency thing a chance.

I stand on the bridge of my ship, gazing into open space. Our scouts said that enemy ships are flooding toward us. They counted four-hundred-fifty. We've brought ourselves up to four-hundred-thirty-eight. It's going to be tough, but we can win this battle.

My chief technician and assistant, a young human girl named Karen, stands beside me. She holds a clipboard in her hand and wears a suit that the Rogue Agency would normally issue to a male officer. The girl's long red hair sways as she turns back toward the other technicians, eyeing a boy in our company by the name of Joss.

Joss doesn't seem to notice, though, turning back to his monitor. I glance over to see what could be so important that he wouldn't notice the girl looking at him. I see, on the screen, lyrics to a song. A human colonial song that I've heard once or twice, being sung by spacers on docks and in bars. "You got a song there, Joss?"

"Yes ma'am, Captain." He nods. "It's a song from... From my colony. I was just looking it back over before the battle."

"Have you got a pair of lungs on you?" I ask him.

He stares at me, befuddled.

"Can you sing?"

"Oh, well, I mean... Not too well, but-"

"Start singing it over the intercom for us." I say, urging him on.

He sighs.

"I don't want to embarrass myself-"

"It's a shanty!" I tell him, patting him on the shoulder. "It doesn't matter if you can sing. Everyone will join in. Come on!"

"Well, alright, Captain." The young brown-headed, spectacled boy looked to his own intercom button. He pressed the button and took a deep breath, readying himself for the song to come.

Eventually, the sound managed to escape his lips. It was light, at first, but it slowly picked up a deepness that carried from person to person, until the whole technician room and likely a good portion of the ship were singing along with him.

When I was a young boy out at sea
My king and country called for me
So I rifle and I wished my best friends well
As I took a nosedive into Hell
Well the war got thick and the waters got still
And we found ourselves in conflict over one small hill
I didn't take favor and I didn't care to take note
So I ran and I hopped onto a boat
With a bag full of ammo and a rifle at my side
I took myself for a wild ride.

Who knows where I'm going, who knows who I'll meet,
Who knows what I'll fail at and who knows what I'll beat
But my heart longs for adventure and my stomach for food
So I'll gain some experience and do the best I can do

Service your country and service yourself
But don't service fame and don't service wealth
My king and country might need me, but I do too
And who knows who I'll meet and what we'll go through?

It's always just seemed more like a rhyme to me than a song, but it catches on. When the song ends, our men and women seem much happier.

Joss goes back to monitoring action, Karen goes back to standing around me waiting for something to say and so on and so forth.

The bridge is spacious, although it's filled with monitors and technicians. The odd soldier or two hangs around, mostly as security, but for the most part the soldiers stand at the cannons, side-blasters and entrance tubes. The engineers work hard to keep the shields at their highest power, and the ship's pub is being worked constantly to keep the off-duty workers happy. The ship's janitors have piled into the pub in high numbers, waiting for this battle to be over with.

It hasn't started yet. We're still waiting in anticipation.

I take a seat at my captain's chair and open up my hologram monitor. I can hear blips coming from the speakers beside my chair as I click various holographic windows with my fingers and examine the words that appear before me.

I decide to give Tom and Jeth'ro a call, so I click the call button. I browse over the varying contacts on the list and click for Tom. I hear a ringing and then an answer.

I can see Golden Tom's face, clear as day. He seems to be covered in make-up, more than usual. A battle, to him, is apparently enough of an occasion that he needs to dress more flamboyantly than usual. He even has the tricorne hat that a stereotypical film pirate would wear. "Ah, Praxis, darling!" He cheers, smiling at me and giving a tip of the hat. "I'm excited for this. Are you excited?"

"Terrified would be a better word." I explain.

He sighs. "It's been a while since I've had a good space battle." He tells me, flashing his unconventionally large blaster-pistol to the camera that I see him on. "Maybe we can board a few of them, and I'll get a chance to use this!"

"Well, Tom, you're thinking positively." I smile. "How's Jeth'ro?"

"Jeth'ro is good!" He tells me, "Do you want to speak to him?"

"Sure."

Tom moves and Jeth'ro's face comes into view moments later. He grins and nods to me. "Praxis, my dear," He starts, "Do you think you'll be using that training I gave you?"

"Probably not." I tell him honestly. "But should I need it, I'll be glad you taught it to me. It's been a pleasure, Jeth'ro. I hope to see you again after this battle."

"And you." He smiles. "I will be fine. But now, I must attend to my duties. The enemy is almost here."

"Alright, Jeth'ro. Goodbye."

"Goodbye."

* * * *

I didn't know what four-hundred-fifty ships at one time would look like. I've learned that it is intimidating, more intimidating than I anticipated.

I still sit in my Captain's chair, seeing no reason to stand. I consider the tactics we can use. I've seen human warships before. They destroyed my home and many faces I once knew were taken aboard them. *You can do this. Just pretend they're Wolfe.*

I press the intercom button on the arm of my chair and lean forward to the microphone that extends just ahead of the chair. "Train cannons on the first row." I say, staring ahead.

I can see ten in a row, flying forward. There are twenty cannons on each side of this ship. "I want this ship turning, starboard side to the enemy."

The engineers and technicians get working and the ship starts to drift in a circular motion until it stops. "Two cannons for every one ship in their front row. I want to break them fast."

My ally ships begin following my command, turning starboard side to the enemy. The enemy is turning as well. As they're turning, we start to unload hell. We're not following any of that 'rules of war' shit. This isn't a game.

The fun thing about human ships is the fact that they don't have shields. Just heavy armor.

I eye each ship in their row. Their bows are turned toward us, but they're starting to move. The bridge rests right on the bow. I can see two shots hit each ship, one right after the other. The back rows are turning, though. They'll engage us soon. Four bridges are disabled within a matter of minutes.

Their ships stop turning, holding up the line. Debris floats from the bows of their ships, forward into the void.

I grin, ordering another round from each cannon.

It isn't long before the front row is completely obliterated. I can see the back row fully turned now, trying to blast their way through the dysfunctional ships. With their blasts being closed off from us, I see an opportunity. "Relay a message to Tom. Tell him to get a handful of ships and move around the enemy's flank."

"Yes ma'am." The message is relayed and it isn't long before Tom's ship starts moving around their own. I can see the name Amelia painted on the side of his ship in bold yellow. He loops his way around them with five other ships as he starts to take their flank. I can see cannons blasting from his end and none firing back. The poor, tactless bastards. Each ship in Tom's cluster focuses on one row, disabling the end ship for each one until they're down to row five.

"I want five ships on the other end. I don't want them getting around." I order.

I'm met with yet another, "Yes ma'am."

The ships begin to drift toward the other side, but I can already see a group of enemies moving in from the left. They meet my other five, and the cannons continue to blast.

Silently, I watch as one of my own ships is conquered in a hailstorm of energy. I watch, I can almost hear the screams as the blast consumes the bridge. Nothing is left of the bow of the ship but debris, much like what we did to the enemy's front row.

Another ship sends out its tubes. It pierces the skin of armor of the one that destroyed our comrade vessel, and the two remain still. The other three on our side begin to fire on the other approaching vessels. I can see Tom in the distance, still laying waste to enemy ships.

"Three small vessels, coming in hot." Yelps one of my technicians.

I shake my head. "Oh no they're not. Fire on them. I want them dead before they even get near us."

Our cannons turn toward them and begin releasing shots. Two go down quickly, but one almost reaches us before our cannon obliterates it. We have strong shields, so it would have taken them a while, but small vessels could still break through our shields if we didn't take them out quickly.

I follow more and more ships breaking through the desolated front row. They turn back toward us as we continue to fire upon them. A row of my own blast and blast, trying not to let them get shots off. There are too many.

Blasts start coming back. The blasts sizzle away as they hit our shields, but nonetheless come close to hitting us.

"Why are those bastards getting shots off? Wipe them out of existence!" I bark.

The blasters start firing faster and faster, roaring and hissing, rattling the ship.

I can see more and more of the enemy die ahead of us, but some of my own ships are falling. Not all of us have the best shields, like mine does. Mine is official Rogue Agency.

I can hear reports coming in from the monitors on the status of everyone else. Tom's report seems to be well, but Alex's report from inside doesn't sound the best.

"They've gotten into the station," Alex's voice says hurriedly, *"But not many. We should be able to take them, if we don't let too many more get in at once."*

His voice leaves the speakers, and I can see more enemy ships roll forward toward us.

I take a deep breath and try to suppress a panic attack, ordering another strike on their line. Their shots retaliate against ours, but in the end, ours prove victorious. We've put far more holes in their ships than they have ours.

I look to Karen, nodding. "Have an ensign bring me some liquor. We're gonna be here for a while." I order.

* * * *

Most of their line has been devastated now. On our side, at least. I can hear Tom's reports rolling in. He's robbing countless ships now that he can do it without suffering shots from surrounding enemy vessels. He's saying he's racked up a total of nineteen-million or so from all of the loot he's gathered.

I'm glad that disease research is going to have such an heavy donation. I'm still fighting with cannons, not trusting the enemy to let them get close enough to board. Every enemy vessel in viewing range is a target. Our cannons crack through the hard shells of their armor and burn away the crew inside.

"When this is over," I announce on a public frequency, so all allies and enemies alike can hear, "I am going to stuff Chandler Bloomfield in an oil drum."

I switch it off of that frequency and focus all of my words on firing orders. I call Pairus on the hologram monitor, hoping to hear some good news from his end. The first thing I hear when he picks up is yelling. "Come on, you son of a whore! My mother fires cannons faster than you!" He turns his focus to me. "Hey, Praxis. All well on your end?"

"We're doing far better than I expected." I answer.

"Good. And, uh, your uh... Your fairy pirate friend, Tom? How's he doing?"

"Tom is destroying them." I answer, a bit offended by his fairy remark. Then, though, I remember that Tom dresses as a colonial gentleman crossed with a surrealist pop star. "Any word on Alex and Taius?"

"Alex is hit pretty bad, but the humans in Proscriptus are in full retreat. Taius took Alex to med-bay. He should be alright there. I also just received word from Allun's hospital." I can feel the strength in his voice retreat. "Someone just tried to pull the plug on Allun. He's alive, but... He's in rough shape. We don't know if he's going to make it."

This was most likely Chandler Bloomfield's work. I'm going to kill that rat bastard.

The battle rages on, bringing down ship after ship until they start to retreat.

"Dock the ship."

* * * *

"Alex," I whimper, rushing into the med bay.

Taius stands by him, holding his hand tight. Alex has a big burn mark on the side of his face, but it's not fatal. Thank God it's not fatal.

A Tartuan doctor runs his scanner over Alex and then starts applying some sort of lotion, which seems to glow green in the near darkness of the med bay. The only light is a black light, probably due to the human assault busting up the power and shutting down most of the main lights in this wing of the station.

"Alex, are you alright?" I feel tears forming.

He smiles at me, releasing Taius' hand and grabbing mine. "Takes more than a few blaster shots to kill me. I'm fine."

He pushes his head back into the pillow, his eyes locking with my own. He closes them as the doctor applies more salve.

"He's lucky the blaster shot only struck the surface. He'll be fine."

* * * *

It's been around three weeks since the battle for Proscriptus. Alex got out of the hospital after the first one, but the blaster did leave a pretty nasty scar on his face.

I've permanently taken the position as a Rogue Agency Captain. Admiral Pairus has granted me the freedom to fly where I wish and do as I see fit, so long as my work falls under the code of the Agency.

Allun has apparently woken up, so I'm going to take my ship to the hospital and say hello before I make Bloomfield disappear. I'm bringing Tom and his crew along, allowing him to loot the office and take what he wishes.

19

Alex

"They fucked me up, kid." I say glumly, staring into the mirror and examining the scar that the damned soldier left on my face. If I'd have caught the bastard, I would have cut open his chest cavity and ripped out his heart.

Praxis' voice erupts from my comm system, although I can only hear part of what she says. Eventually the static smooths out and I can actually make out most of her words.

She may not have heard mine, though, so I repeat myself. "They fucked me up. I thought I was ugly enough as it was."

I try to turn things around, learning to laugh at myself. I stand in Taius' penthouse lounge, all by myself. Only two nameless guards keep me company, as well as an Astarian slave that sweeps up the floor around me.

"I think they may have un-fucked me," She laughs back, although it's mostly grating static that accompanies the humor.

I look at the crater in my face that leaves a big green scar around my pale red skin. Come to think of it, I never noticed how pale red my skin is. I'm almost pink, like Praxis. Jesus, that makes me feel a lot less masculine. How the hell does a pink guy intimidate anyone?

"I feel a lot better about this Rogue Agency thing. It's giving me a more optimistic outlook on things right now."

"Well one of us has to have optimism." I speak into my watch, turning away from the mirror and over to the window.

I can see the void of space in all her majesty. My god, she *is* majestic, too. I wonder what kind of worlds are out there that we haven't found. I have the passing thought to become a spacer, but I throw that thought out just as soon as it comes. I'm not going to be a spacer. I don't need to be a spacer and I don't want to be. "It ain't me and it sure as shit ain't Allun. How's the man doing, anyhow?"

"Wouldn't know. Haven't gotten to him yet."

This disappoints me a bit. I'd like to know how my brother is doing, but I'm sure he feels the same way. I wonder if anyone even told him that we won the fight.

"You know, Alex, I think I might actually use this Rogue Agency thing to my advantage. Explore the galaxy. Pairus tells me I don't even have to stick with his fleet. I just need to support him when he calls for me. Apart from that, I'm free to go anywhere."

"Well I hear that a lot of the outer worlds are beautiful this time of year," I smile and think about how fulfilled Praxis seems.

I know I'm not her dad, but she's still my child. Her happiness still makes me happy. Her success is my success. Damn it, I never thought I'd feel so strongly about anyone I wasn't related to. "Some of them won't even hit winter for another five-hundred years. You know how weird season changes between worlds are."

"Alex? Are you doing alright? You haven't been an asshole all night." She jests and I laugh, leaning against the wall and feeling myself begin to tear, I'm getting old and soft. It won't be long before I'm dead, at the rate I'm going. Five-hundred years is a long time. My brothers will live that long. My mom will, my sisters, my aunts--I'm going to be dead before then. Am I even a relative to them? Or just a pet? Jesus Christ, I don't want to end up being the family dog. I don't want to live and die like this only to get replaced a few years later. "You know, Praxis... That

fight showed me just how close to death I am. If an outside source doesn't kill me, my own age is going to hit me soon enough. I don't have much time left, kiddo."

"Don't talk like that," She argues, *"You're going to live a nice, full life and you've still got plenty ahead of you. How old are you? Fifty? Fifty-five?"*

"Sixty-four." I grumble, not wanting to be reminded of my own age.

God, that battle... I can still feel it. The heat of the blast. The burning, the stinging, the screaming. I remember going under before the battle ended. I remember the last thing I saw being Taius storming over to me, rifle in hand, in his old uniform with his old medals on his chest. He was fighting with all his might to preserve me from their blasts.

"Look, kid, I'm going to bed. Love ya."

"I love you too, Alex. Good night."

* * * *

"Breach in the station! Breach in the station!"

I can still hear the screaming. The crier yelped and ran, alerting all of the citizens and soldiers of the station's west wing. The siren he carried blared as he swept down the wide metal halls, screeching and howling like a madman.

Taius and I stood with our lines of men, some of our men in front with blaster-proof shields while some of us in the back walked with rifles.

Taius and I walked in the very back, carrying our old war rifles.

White metal surrounded us. The west wing always was the least decorative. The crier kept running beyond us, and we took our wall position once more, slowly moving forward. We cut off the intercom systems to keep the shields powered, but it obviously didn't do a very good job in assisting us.

"These men are after your freedom and your lives." Taius growled and took a gulp from his water skin, another old military tool of his. He loves it when he gets opportunities to use that old shit.

He raised the rifle and aimed it over the shoulders of the men in front of him, who aimed their rifles over the shoulders of the men in front of them and so on until finally they go over the shield carriers' shoulders.

"They want to destroy us. Not just us, the Vortigans, but all who rally under the Vortigan banner. All who bow to our name and draw guns and blades in our honor. You know what they're going to do if they take Proscriptus? They're going to rape all of the women on the station, starting with the female soldiers. I've seen enough invasions in my time to know that this is the kind of shit that happens when dealing with humans. First, they rape your wives, girlfriends, mistresses, sisters and daughters; then they'll take your sons, brothers, husbands and boyfriends and either kill them or sell them to their colonies as field workers."

Telling them this seemed to put them in a fighting mood. Ignoring the fact that Tartarus does the same thing, that was a pretty good tactic for getting the fighting men and women of Proscriptus to raise arms.

Our force pressed on, our guns all pointing down the hall. Not a single human soldier was going to get past us without getting at least a few holes in them, if they passed us at all. Human soldiers are so tactless, most likely *we* would be passing over *them*--their scorched corpses, that is.

We kept marching until the first wave came in. Eight human soldiers were on the move, so there weren't very many at first. They must have moved ahead of the rest, I decided before ordering the wall down. Our fifty blasters gunned down their eight without a single hint of resistance.

Our black boots stomped over the bodies of our fallen enemies as we pressed on. Ten more soldiers sprinted for us. One hand signal and the shields went down. The barrels of the front row's guns blasts sizzling blue shots of energy, burning through chests, necks and heads. A single shot managed to enter the crowd, and a member of our front row went down with a scream. The man behind him stepped up to take his place and the men pressed together, just as tight as before.

I looked down at our fallen comrade and sighed, knowing that it would probably be me telling his next of kin of his sacrifice.

Twenty more were ahead now, forming their own line. Our shields stood high, but the enemy soldiers saw a weakness. The feet of our shield-carriers were vulnerable. A few rounds went off at their feet and a few went down, leaving a good portion of us open.

We began firing, falling back with what was left of our shield wall. I, personally, brought down four. I saw six more go down before we'd fallen back. Our screaming allies were shot dead before, us and we found ourselves shooting faster and with even more malice behind our shots.

We easily brought down the rest of their force before going any farther. Most of the rooms to our sides had sealed doors, but some of them may have been kicked in or unlocked.

I could hear the crying of a Sprite girl as she was being assaulted and the screams of Tartuan women as their husbands were butchered. Our men began pouring into the open rooms, wasting the intruders.

A few civilian men and women joined us, carrying their own rifles, pistols and shotguns. A fifteen-year-old Alkin girl walked alongside a century old Tartuan whore, the two of them fighting with fierceness and camaraderie to defend Proscriptus. Even the Space-Born slaves stood side-by-side with their masters, probably in what was the only time they've ever held or ever will hold guns.

I saw a human soldier with a cut throat lying in the hall, alongside a half-naked dead woman with a knife. She died fighting. Poor woman.

I blasted every human soldier around them, burning through flesh and bone in an attempt to gain some sort of retaliation against these bastards. A young woman in a Vortigan soldier uniform walked with me, her eyes blazing as the enemy soldiers died at the end of her barrel. Damn, do I want that girl at my back if I ever need backup again. She and I stopped in a civilian's room where couches and tables had been flipped to shield from blasters.

A young couple died there hand in hand, each one clutching their own pistol.

The girl smiled at me, reaching down into her pocket and drawing a flask, taking a long gulp. She offered it to me and I gratefully accepted, drinking like a fish. The whiskey was bitter, but I didn't mind. It still helped me out quite a bit.

"So you been in a lot of battles?" She asked me, eyeing me up and down. She was far too young for me, probably around nineteen or twenty, but I wasn't going to tell her to stop looking.

I shook my head, leaning against the wall and lighting myself one of Allun's cigarettes. "I try to stay out of them, but sometimes you just can't avoid it. Remember the Alkin Invasion?" I asked, wondering if she's ever even seen the world where we originated. She shrugged, though I know she heard about it. It was big news all throughout the galaxy for years after it happened.

"I got myself into a shootout with some human soldiers back then. Had to smuggle me and Praxis off-world. You met Praxis?" I asked.

Seeing as she was assigned to Proscriptus, she very well may have met the girl. "Oh, that hot piece of ass? The things I would-

"She's been like a daughter to me," I interrupted, not wanting to hear the rest of that. "I'd prefer you not tell me what you'd do to her."

"R-right, sorry." She began to blush, looking away. She eyed the kitchen of the dead couple's apartment, looking over the three human bodies left there. "We're really giving them hell, huh?"

"Damn right." I smiled, nodded and headed back into the action.

The girl stayed in the apartment, probably for the remainder of the battle, while I ran back with the men.

Our troops were less organized now that our formation was broken. We ran wild, blasting holes into the human soldiers that remained. It was right when I got back to the action that I found myself wounded.

The bastards blindsided me. I heard a sizzle; I felt a burning that was small at first, but grew and grew until finally the pain overcame me. I screamed and fell, clutching my face.

I could see Taius in the distance as I rolled over, looking to my men. They were forming a wall around my front. Taius rushed forward, a genuine worry and sadness in his eyes. He was shocked. So was I.

I closed my eyes and passed out, although I could still feel the burning. It was so prominent, even in my sleep. I dreamt of Hell that night.

20

Allun

"Well ain't you a sight for sore eyes," I smile, seeing Praxis enter my cell of the hospital room.

I sit upright, no longer having the tubes stuffed in my orifices. I'm close to leaving. All I need to do is sign the release papers.

I notice something different about Praxis' attire--I notice a uniform, not just a suit. She wears a Rogue Agency Captain's uniform. The only uniform in the galaxy that resembles true freedom. The uniform in the galaxy I respect more than any other.

"What brings you to my shitty little prison this... evening?"

"It's morning." She says, looking to my window.

I can't even tell. I can't reach the window, and the curtain is so dark I can't see the time of day. "Why are you in a room like this? You're a Vortigan family head."

"That doesn't mean shit here." I growl. "And, um... I may have caused them a bit of trouble and they had to... Deadbolt me in here."

She approaches the bed, grinning. "You ready to leave here?"

"Can you pull some strings? I don't feel like doing the paperwork."

* * * *

"So where are we going?" I ask her, walking toward the spaceport and lighting a cigarette, courtesy of Praxis.

The streets are bustling, full of life. A young Sprite courier rushes by us, a sash slung over his shoulder. He waves down a taxi and swings the door open, jumping in. The air out here is cleaner than air on Tartarus, although the heat is just as bad. On the bright side, you can actually see the sky. It's a bright blue sky that hangs above the city, covered in white clouds with a big yellow sun lingering alongside them. People here, despite the benefits of living on a world that's actually clean for the most part, seem to think that being abrasive and rude is still necessary. I can't speak, though. I'm just as abrasive as these people.

"We're going to go find Chandler Bloomfield," She tells me, stopping at a crosswalk and smiling back at me, "And we're going to make him wish he was dead."

I like the sound of that. We'll pull the plug on that prick the same way he pulled it on me. The difference here is that we're actually going to make sure he's dead. That's something he failed to do upon our first meeting.

"I've got a privateer friend who gets to loot his office while we deal with him, so don't smash it up too much." She leads me into the spaceport and we meet with who I assume is her friend, a flamboyant man with golden blond hair and covered in makeup. Not the weirdest thing I've seen in my lifetime. Alongside him is a white-winged Delkyrian with a sword at his hip.

Praxis talks quietly with them both while I lean back against a crate, awaiting their meeting to end.

The two walk back to me with her, both reaching out to shake my hand. I shake them both politely, giving each one a nod.

The Delkyrian is fucking ripped and apparently doesn't mind showing it. He doesn't seem to like shirts much, given he isn't wearing one despite being in a crowded city where clothes would usually be considered polite to wear.

"Golden Tom," the privateer nods to me, "at your service."

"Jeth'ro." The Delkyrian says, turning to the road. "Come on. I am excited." He speaks in English, but it's broken. It's *extremely* broken. Still, I can make out what he's saying and the emotions he's attempting to convey.

The four of us walk in a square on the sidewalk until we find ourselves outside of what I assume is the city's capitol building. Chandler Bloomfield is the city's representative, so it would make sense for his office to be here. Outside of the capitol is a statue of a horse, crafted from fine marble, with a few trees in a circle of grass around it. The capitol itself is probably hundreds of years old, also crafted with marble for the steps and floors.

We make our way through, brushing off any security by flashing Praxis' badge. Eventually we reach a large set of wooden double-doors with the name 'Bloomfield' written on a plaque just to the right of them.

Praxis nods to me. I nod back and she swings open the doors. Two security guards rush forward, but back off when they see her badge. It's nice to be in company of Rogue Agency. Anything goes.

"Security, out." She orders and they listen. They rush outside, closing the doors behind them.

Bloomfield sits at his desk, staring at the four of us in sheer terror.

"R-Rogue Agency?" He says, his nasally and high-pitched voice as annoying as it was when we first met. "There were Rogue Agency ships at the battle, according to the report. I don't... I don't understand. What Rogue Agency laws have I personally broken?" He's shaking in his boots.

Praxis reaches down to her second holster and hands me a blaster. Hopefully she'll let me do the honors when we actually execute him. We're going to invoke some fear first.

"The first and foremost--do not cause war, especially not on a galactic scale." She informs him, taking a seat at the desk across from him. She leans forward, grinning and staring him in the eyes. "Do you have a money vault in this office?" She asks.

He shakes his head.

"If you're lying, I'm going to shoot you in the head."

"O-Over there." He pulls a key from his drawer, handing it to her.

She tosses it to Tom, who follows Chandler's pointing finger to the portrait on the wall. He rips down the portrait, sliding the key into the lock and pulling out stacks and stacks of cash. Jeth'ro holds open a sack for it as Tom drops it in.

"I... I didn't know that was the law. I'm... Truly sorry. It won't happen again."

"No, Mr. Bloomfield." Praxis says coldly. "It won't. Do you know the Rogue Agency's punishment for war-mongering?"

"I'm not familiar." He gulps, blinking rapidly and looking between Praxis, Tom, Jeth'ro and me.

"Whatever punishment a captain decides." She presses her blaster to his forehead, pushing until he's forced against the back of his chair.

He quivers, shaking his head.

"You wanted a war with the Vortigans. You lost the first battle and these are the repercussions. Do you understand?"

"P-please, I... I have kids. I have a wife. My career was... My career just got started ten years ago. I don't want to die just yet."

He's starting to tear up. The poor, dumb bastard thinks we're going to show him mercy. As if we haven't taken the chance of widowing wives and orphaning children with every kill in the past.

"Sometimes," I say, "The family is better without a member."

I train my gun on his chest. I don't want to give him the release of a quick death. Not after what he did to me and tried to do to my family. "Don't worry," I grin, coming around the back of his desk and putting my hand on his shoulder, still aiming the gun for his chest. "We'll spare your family."

I aim the gun slightly down, so that it's pointing at his balls.

He clenches his eyes shut, and I tilt it slightly upward, letting off a shot. It hits his desk, but it's enough to scare him into covering his genitals. "No!" He screams, flailing like a maniac.

I punch him across the face to stop his incessant flopping, putting my hand on his throat. He calms down quick. That punch would probably leave a black eye, if we were going to leave his face recognizable. "I know I wronged you, I'm sorry! Take my money! My valuables! Just don't kill me!"

"We're taking your money and your valuables." I say, "Your valuables including your life. Think about the headlines. 'Chandler Bloomfield Found Mutilated.' What about 'Chandler Bloomfield Commits Suicide'?"

"I'm not going to kill myself!" He argues. "Not if you do it."

Praxis pulls her gun away from his forehead, and I notice a circle from where the barrel was pressed. I press my own barrel over it, aligning it perfectly.

I pull the trigger, searing through his head and leaving nothing but ash within it. I drop the blaster on his desk and turn toward the door, waving Praxis and the others back over.

"Get the rest of the valuables and let's go." I order, but Praxis interjects.

"You don't give the orders anymore." She growls. "I do."

I want to be mad, but I honestly can't. I'm proud of the kid. She's sticking up for herself, she's taking charge and, most of all, she's right. Rogue Agency overrules all. I can't give her orders if she doesn't allow it.

I lean against the wall and smile at her. "You're gonna go far, kid."

* * * *

Next on our list are the Dreadwal brothers.

It's been about a nineteen hour flight going the highest speed to Sar Drea in Praxis' Rogue Agency warship. Golden Tom's ship hasn't been far behind us, with Jeth'ro and Praxis conversing a lot via holographic monitor the entire way.

Praxis contacted Torius Dreadwal hours prior to our arrival to meet her on the docks with the brothers in cuffs. He sounded saddened to do it, but he knows his own laws and the Rogue Agency's. They assisted in war-mongering, so they pay the price.

Our ship flies into the docks of Sar Drea and, while it isn't home, I still feel happy in the knowledge that I'm on Tartarus. Our ship docks and I follow Praxis out of the doors and onto the docks. I see another truck full of slaves being dragged away, as I did back in Sar Vort daily, as well as an auction stage toward the end of the dock. An auction is currently in progress, but our sights are set on two bigger fish.

The brothers are in cuffs, just as requested, with guards holding them for us. Their father stands in the back, watching solemnly.

Praxis stands before the boys, looking to their father. I look to him as well. My boys were never as shitty as these two, but I still know what it's like to lose your kids. Despite what I thought previously, I take no pleasure in this.

Praxis points her guns for the oldest of the two, who barks like a madman. "For the crime of war-mongering," She sighs, "I sentence you to death."

She shoots him in the head then turns to the other. He flails and screams, being held in place by one of his own guards.

"When I get out of these cuffs, I'm going to rape you, you fucking-"

His words are cut off by a blaster shot. Both boys' faces are unrecognizable now.

The guards look back to their boss, who closes his eyes and takes a deep breath. I can see tears breaking through. "My boys were monsters." He whimpers. "But they were my children. I raised them. I loved them, no matter what. I..."

"I know." I say to him, thinking back to Walder.

I should make peace with Taius. I should. Part of me doesn't want to, though. Of course, the other part of me says fuck that part, he's your brother. My mind is so conflicted. I'll figure it out eventually. "Is your wife still living?" I ask.

He shakes his head. "No, but she just rolled over in her grave."

21

Praxis

The forest is a grim sight. Bodies hang in the tall green trees that surround me. Alkin bodies hang alongside Tartuan indiscriminately. The sun hovers in the sky above the forest, staring down on the chaos of the world's surface.

I can hear footsteps crunch leaves and twigs behind me. It's distant at first, but soon the storm of cracks and crunches is so close it almost feels as if it's coming from within my own head.

I turn to see a face I once knew; a face I thought meant nothing to me anymore. I see the face of Zeph. His body is twisted atrociously, his head being the only part of him that seems to stay consistently aimed for me. His dead eyes follow my every motion, his fingernails and mouth caked with blood. He still has the same soft but strong face he had all those years ago, still youthful and stupid. I can see the guilt on his face. The dumb bastard was the reason we were ever separated in the first place. He hasn't aged a day, but I suppose corpses don't.

He grabs for me with bloody hands, causing me to recoil in fear.

I swat at him, taking a few steps back.

He grabs again and I punch him square in the nose, but it doesn't seem to do much good. He clutches my wrist, his grip tightening.

I can feel my skin break under his pressure. I take two fingers and ram them into his eye sockets, causing his eyeballs to pop like water balloons. I pull my hand back, disgusted at the sight and feeling of Zeph's blood squirting out onto me and soaking my hand.

The blue blood sprays out onto my face and I scream, punching again at the face that now runs blue. He looks like Oedipus Rex with that blood seeping down from his eyes. He releases my wrist and wails like a banshee, giving me time to run.

I sprint into the thick woods, keeping my eye on a distant light. A gorgeous clearing, just out of my reach. I can hear the crackling of more leaves far behind me.

I look back to see his arms limp and his legs moving unnaturally, carrying him along. He seems to hop the logs and make it through the bushes with no trouble, still running closely behind me.

I can feel his blood seeping down my hand and mixing with my own from where he grabbed me and dug his claws in. He roars ferociously as he catches up behind me, still swiping for me.

I run faster, tiring my legs more quickly but carrying me more distance. I suddenly feel myself consumed in blinding light. I keep running until I regain my vision.

I'm in a field of flowers now, just beyond the forest itself. Zeph screams as the light hits him and he collapses, screaming in agony as the sun burns away his flesh.

His blood evaporates from his own body and my hand, causing me to feel a sense of pride when I look back. The field is sunny and gorgeous, with a big blue sky above me.

The sun stares down at me proudly as ships begin to move into view. Warships begin to descend, but I feel no fear. I feel no anger. I feel pride. I feel happiness. I feel alive.

I feel awake now.

* * * *

"Praxis," Jeth'ro says as I run my fingers through his hair.

We lie in bed on my ship, in the docks of Proscriptus. The lights are dark, as they were the first time we made love. I have my arm around him and his head on my chest, as I have before.

The sound in his voice is sullen. He carries bad news with just his tone. "Tomorrow, I leave with Tom once more on a privateering voyage. We will not see each other again for a long time." He informs me, but I focus on those key words: 'for a long time.'

"But we will see each other again." I say to him, smiling.

I don't think any man's company has made me as happy as his so far. I honestly think I might love him. The problem with that is that neither of us have time for love. He's a privateer, and I'm a Rogue Agency captain. He has ships to rob, and I have worlds to liberate. I kiss him warmly, softly and passionately--I don't want to release the kiss.

"You said before, we have separate paths. That doesn't mean they won't rejoin eventually."

"I'll visit when I can." He tells me.

I smile even wider.

He adds, "We'll have to visit Seregua together some day."

"We will." I close my eyes and lay my head back against the pillow.

"So what will you do next?"

"Anything I want, I guess."

THE END

About The Author

Seventeen-year-old author, Robert Midgett, has been writing since third grade. After his teacher ripped his story up in front of him, stating it was too violent, he had a little rebellion kick in. At 11, he wrote a screenplay that he would rather no one ever read. Lessons were learned and at 13, he began writing his first published novel. 'Vagabonds' was born and it took two years to grow into the Science Fiction novel that movies are made from. From Bradbury to Lovecraft to Twain to McKim, his writing influences are wide-spread. Robert decided, early-on, that he would give back by donating 10% of his profit from his novel to St. Jude Children's Hospital, showing that his heart is as big as his imagination. All the way from the small town of Mount Juliet, Tennessee, meet Robert Midgett.

www.ingramcontent.com/pod-product-compliance
Lightning Source LLC
Chambersburg PA
CBHW050451110726
47899CB00003B/898